PUBLISHER'S NOTE

This is the fourth volume of Charlie Small's journal and it was found under even more [un]ual circumstances than normal! The publishers were informed through the website, [c]harliesmall.co.uk, of a possible sighting of Charlie. Excitedly, one of our intrepid [ ] packed her bags and by plane, hot-air balloon and donkey, travelled to the valley [C]harlie had last been seen. He wasn't there. Our agent searched high and low, and [st]ill, but could not find him. She did meet a skinny gunslinger in a bar who, when [j]ust spat and said he'd never heard of Charlie Small. But our editor had already [s][ ] a familiar-looking notebook propped behind a whisky bottle and when the outlaw's [ba][ ]as turned, she slipped it in her pocket and left.

[ ]is the journal that was hidden behind the bottles. It proves beyond a doubt that [Ch][ ]e Small is still out there, still having adventures. There must be more notebooks to [fin][ ] if you do come across a curious-looking diary, or see a boy who is an expert with [a la][ ], please do contact us via the Charlie Small website.

[ ]at any time, you are challenged to a gunfight by a skinny young Desperado, just say no. I've heard he is as fast as a rattlesnake!)

A[D]DRESS: *Destiny*

A[G]E: 400 (maybe even more)

M[O]BILE: 07713 122[ ]

I used to go to

[SCH]OOL: St Beckham's, a long time ago

[THIN]GS I LIKE: Gorillas, swinging through [tree]s; my hammock aboard the 'Betty Mae';
p[ract]ising cutlass fighting; Braemar; Jenny a[nd] anny Green

THINGS I HATE: Joseph Craik (a bully);
Captain [ ];
The Pu[ ]c[ ]ck swabbing;
being [ ]S

Yeehah!

THE AMAZING ADVENTURES OF CHARLIE SMALL (400)

MARSHAL

Notebook 4

DESTINY MOUNTAIN

d b
FICKLING
David Fickling Books

CHARLIE SMALL JOURNAL 4: DESTINY MOUNTAIN
A DAVID FICKLING BOOK
978 0 385 61730 7

Published in Great Britain by David Fickling Books,
a division of Random House Children's Books
A Random House Group Company
First published as *The Daredevil Desperados of Destiny* 2008

This edition published 2009

1 3 5 7 9 10 8 6 4 2

The Random House Group Limited makes every effort to ensure that the papers used in its books are
made from trees that have been legally sourced from well-managed and credibly certified forests.
Our paper procurement policy can be found at: www.randomhouse.co.uk/paper.htm

Mixed Sources
Product group from well-managed
forests and other controlled sources
www.fsc.org Cert no. TT-COC-2139
© 1996 Forest Stewardship Council
FSC

Set in 15/17 Garamond MT

DAVID FICKLING BOOKS
31 Beaumont Street, Oxford, OX1 2NP

www.rbooks.co.uk

Addresses for companies within The Random House Group Limited can be found at:
www.randomhouse.co.uk/offices.htm

THE RANDOM HOUSE GROUP Limited Reg. No. 954009

A CIP catalogue record for this book is available from the British Library.

Printed in the UK by CPI Bookmarque, Croydon, CR0 4TD

If you find this book, PLEASE look after it. This is the only true account of my remarkable adventures.

   My name is Charlie Small and I am four hundred years old, maybe even more. But in all those long years I have never grown up. Something happened when I was eight years old, something I can't begin to understand. I went on a journey... and I'm still trying to find my way home. Now, although I have destroyed a terrible two-headed vulture, robbed a bank and been caught in the middle of a bison stampede, I still look like any eight-year-old you might pass in the street.

   I've travelled to the ends of the earth and to the centre of the earth. I've been chased by a merciless posse, I've really rattled a rattlesnake and caught a cougar by the tail! You may think this sounds fantastic; you could think it's a lie. But you would be wrong, because EVERYTHING IN THIS BOOK IS TRUE. Believe this single fact and you can share the most incredible journey ever experienced!

Charlie Small

Wild
Bob
Ffrance

Looking Down The Barrel
Of A Colt 45

BUMP!

'Ouch!' I cried as I rolled to a stop. Looking back I could see that I had tumbled down a huge gorge between two cliff walls. The ground beneath me was dusty and scrubby, and I was just about to get up and dust myself down, when I heard a familiar click behind my left ear.

'Where d'ya think you're goin', boy?' asked a soft voice. I turned around carefully, with my arms raised, and found myself staring down the barrel of a Colt 45.

'Oh, shucks! It's a bad day for you, boy,' said the young man looking at me. Piercing blue eyes shone from a dirty, grimy face; his long, greasy hair hung down to his shoulders, and he had the meanest grin I've ever seen.

'I'm Wild Bob Ffrance, the most wanted outlaw in the whole of the wild and wicked west – and you've just barged into my camp.'

Oh no! Help!

Things Go From Bad To Worse

With a twitch of his pistol, he signalled me towards a campfire that glowed behind some scrubby bushes, and from where the smell of cooking drifted.

'Hands behind your head, boy, and no funny business or I'll splatter your brains on the ground like a mess of baked beans.'

I did as I was told! I put up my hands and walked towards the fire, expecting to hear the bang of his gun and feel the sting of a bullet between my shoulder blades at any second.

This is just typical, I said to myself. There you were, safe and sound and living the life of a hero with old Granny Green, when you decide you want to go exploring again; then you want to find your way back home. And before the end of the very same day, here you are being marched at gunpoint by a crazy, trigger-happy cowboy. Brilliant!

'Turn around. Now, sit down on that rock and keep quiet,' said Wild Bob Ffrance, and again I did exactly as I was told. Well, almost!

'Look, I'm no threat to you,' I began to say.

'I just stumbled down . . .'

P'TANG! Wild Bob's gun spat a tongue of orange flame and a bullet ricocheted off the rock where I sat. *P'tang . . . p'tang . . . p'tang!* The sound echoed across the evening sky.

'What part of "sit down and keep quiet" do you not understand?' said the man, spitting into the dirt at his feet.

'Well, I . . .'

P'TANG! Another bullet chipped the rock, just by my left hand, stinging my fingers. OK, I got the message!

'Now, let's see what you've got in there,' he said, pointing to my rucksack. 'Hand it over, nice and easy.'

Accused

PTANG!

The outlaw took my rucksack, his gun still trained on me, and tipped it up. My telescope and magnifying glass, the maps, my journal and all the other paraphernalia, fell to the ground.

'It's my explorer's kit,' I said helpfully.

'It looks like a spy's kit to me,' said the gunman through gritted teeth. 'You were sent by Horatio Ham to spy on me, weren't you, you low-down dog.'

'Ham! Who's Horatio Ham? I'm just trying to . . .'

'Shut your jabbering, boy,' the cowboy replied. 'I know a sneaking, slinking spy when I see one. Well, you've been spying on the wrong man this time.' He flicked open the chamber on his pistol and started reloading it with bullets from his gun belt.

Charlie

↖ A bullet with my name on it!

Yikes! Was this going to be the end of all my adventures?

Challenged

'Hold on a minute,' I said. My heart was thumping so hard I thought it might burst out of my chest. 'What are you doing?'

'Don't worry, Mister Spy,' said the outlaw, clicking his gun shut. 'I'm not a murderer. It's going to be a fair fight; don't let anybody say that Wild Bob isn't fair. I'm challenging you to a fastest-to-the-draw gunfight!'

Fair! Who was he trying to kid?

'I can't use a gun,' I cried, very scared indeed. 'I've never even held one before.'

'Don't give me that. Everybody knows how to use a gun. Why, I was given one as a christening present!'

'Well, I was given a silver napkin ring for mine,' I said. 'I really don't know how to use a gun. So, sorry, but I'm afraid I can't fight you!'

Wild Bob Ffrance stared at me for a moment, then smiled and put his gun down on a rock. Phew! I thought. I've got out of that one!

'OK. Maybe you can't fight with a gun,' said Ffrance. 'So, I'll make it easy for you; follow me.' And he led me into a clearing by the cliff where I had fallen. It was scarred with cracks and caves of all shapes and sizes.

The outlaw turned his back to the cliff and faced me. 'If you can't use a gun, you'll have to use something else,' he said. 'So, choose your weapon, boy; any weapon you like.'

With that, he took a huge Bowie knife from his boot and sent it juddering into a nearby tree. Before it had even finished vibrating, he pulled a slingshot from his pocket and launched a stone through the air, knocking a crow from the branch of a cactus plant; finally, he unfurled a long leather whip from his belt and flicking it with a loud crack, plucked the knife back out of the tree; the knife span up into the air, and he casually caught it in his free hand. 'What's it to be, boy?' he asked.

Boing!

I was done for. This outlaw was a phenomenon! He was an expert with a gun, a knife, a slingshot, a whip and who knows what else? I wasn't an expert at anything. (Well that's not entirely true; the Perfumed Pirates of Perfidy had taught me to be an expert sword fighter.)

'Do you have any cutlasses?' I asked, praying that he would say no so I didn't have to fight.

'Not much call for cutlasses in the Wild West,' replied Ffrance, and spat on the ground. 'You'll have to choose something else.'

It was obvious that he wasn't going to let me off and I was going to have to fight. But what else was I good at? It was then I noticed the lasso, curled around the pommel of a black leather saddle that had been placed in the shade of the cliff face.

Well, I was good at swinging through trees and climbing the rigging of a pirate ship. I was an expert at dangling from the end of puppet strings; I had become very good with all sorts of rope on my various adventures. Maybe I would be good with a lasso as well! There was only one way to find out. I pointed at the rope.

'The lasso?' asked the outlaw. I nodded. 'So, you're a rope merchant, are you?' And he tossed the coil of rope to me.

The Fight

'Oooof!' The weight of the lasso knocked me to the ground, and Wild Bob Ffrance smiled as I struggled back to my feet. This was ridiculous. How on earth was I supposed to throw the lasso when I could hardly lift it up?

'It looks like you're having a bit of trouble, boy,' chuckled Wild Bob. 'So, just to make things a bit fairer, I'm gonna fight you barehanded . . . with one arm behind my back . . . standing on one leg . . . and with one eye closed!'

I think he was starting to find me a bit of a joke!

'Ready?' he asked. I unfurled the coil of rope until I found the loop of the lasso, and started to swing it over my head like I'd seen the cowboys do on telly.

'Ready!' I cried, but the rope got tangled around my arms, slipped down over my head and ended up curling around my ankles. I toppled over once again.

Wild Bob smiled as I scrambled to my feet once more. 'Are you ready now?' he asked again. 'Now, FIGHT!'

And he hopped towards me on one leg, while looking through one eye. He should have looked ridiculous, but he looked as mean as a wild cat.

Clumsily, I swung the rope and threw it, hoping that somehow the loop would fall around the outlaw and I could bring him down . . . but it went sailing off in completely the wrong direction!

What happened next happened very, very fast!

As I threw the lasso, I saw to my horror that

the mouth of the cave right behind Wild Bob Ffrance was suddenly filled by the biggest, sleepiest and grumpiest grizzly bear I've ever seen. As my lasso sailed away in the wrong direction, the grizzly bear raised his huge paws above Wild Bob's head and gave an ear-shattering roar. Instantly, the outlaw dropped to one knee, turning to face the grizzly and going for his gun at the same time. But his gun wasn't there; it still sat on the rock where he had left it with his other weapons.

The ghastly Grizzly bear.

The bear began to lumber towards the defenceless outlaw. At the same instant my wayward lasso fell onto Ffrance's revolver, sending it clattering from the rock. The gun hit the ground and went off. P'TANG! The bullet hit the rocks above the mouth of the cave, and a lump of granite the size of a pineapple fell straight onto the grizzly's head with a sickening *crack!*

The bear stopped in his tracks. He blinked once; he blinked twice, and slowly went cross-eyed. With a huge sigh, like a deflating bouncy castle, he dropped down onto all fours. Wild Bob rushed to get his gun, but the grizzly bear had ambled away in a complete daze. He didn't know what day it was any more!

'WOW! That was some mighty fancy rope work, boy,' said Wild Bob. 'You saved my skin and no mistake, even if you are a spy for Horatio Ham.'

'Oh, it's OK,' I said nonchalantly. 'But I am not a spy for Horatio Ham, honest I'm not. My name is Charlie Small, and I'm just a boy who's trying to get home.'

'I think I believe you; but don't you know it's not safe to be wandering through this territory while Ham is about?' said Bob. 'I think you'd better stick with me for the time being.' And the young man came striding over to me and shook my hand. 'You've just made a friend for life, Charlie Small; and after the way you lassoed my pistol, I'm going to call you the Lariat Kid from now on.'

'What's a lariat?' I asked.

'A lariat is another word for a lasso,' said Wild

Bob. 'I thought you would have known that, being an expert and all.'

'Oh yes, lariat. I remember now,' I said, quickly.

Wild Bob chuckled. 'Whatever,' he said. 'Now, let's go and see if my supper is ready.'

Wild Bob's Fireside Story

Now I'm ready for bed, camping out under a large, pale moon that floats in an indigo sky. My head is spinning from Wild Bob's tales, and I'm writing up my journal before I go to sleep.

Earlier today, back in Wild Bob's camp, I collected up the bits and pieces of my explorer's kit, checking they were all there as I put them back into my rucksack.

1) My multi-tooled penknife
2) A ball of string
3) A water bottle
   (full to the brim once more)
4) A telescope
5) A scarf

COMPLIMENTARY

TICKET TO ANYWHERE
ONE WAY OR ANOTHER

DATE:
ANYTIME

16 2973

6) An old railway ticket

7) This journal

8) A pack of wild animal collector's cards

9) A glue pen (to stick any interesting finds in my book)

10) A glass eye from the steam-powered rhinoceros

11) The hunting knife, the compass and torch I found on the sun-bleached skeleton of a lost explorer

Life size drawing

Razor sharp for easy slicing!

12) The tooth of a monstrous river crocodile
13) A magnifying glass
14) A radio
15) My mobile phone with wind-up charger
16) The skull of a Barbarous Bat
17) A bundle of maps, collected during my travels
18) A few doubloons from the *Betty Mae*

I have lost some things on my journey (my pyjamas had been shredded by the giant snow worms; Jenny and I scoffed the Paterchak mint humbugs and Kendal mint cake as soon as we had freed ourselves from our puppet prison; the large slab of whale meat was devoured by Braemar, the white wolf) but I replaced them with equally useful stuff from the store in the village where Jenny and her grandmother live.

19) A bag of marbles
20) An automatic travel umbrella
21) A large slab of Granny Green's toffee
22) A plastic lemon full of lemon juice.
(A squirt of lemon juice can make the most disgusting ingredients just about edible!)

A useful collection of things, I think you'll agree.

A plastic squirty lemon.

Then, as coyotes howled in the distance and the tumbleweed rustled in the breeze, Wild Bob handed me a delicious plate of beans and bacon. As we ate, he told me the story of how he had become an outlaw. I soon realized he was as innocent of being a bandit as I was of being a piratical terror on the high seas.

(See my journal Pirate Galleon)

It all began a long time ago when Bob was about eight years old. His mum and dad had a small farm called Two-Eyes. They had a very happy life until, one day, a man called Horatio Ham bought the rest of the land in the valley and started up as a cattle rancher.

Now Ham was a bully, pure and simple, and he wanted to own the whole valley, especially the river that tumbled out of the surrounding hills and flowed straight through the Ffrance farm. If he owned the river he could control the supply of water to the nearby town of Trouble, and therefore the town itself.

First he tried to buy the farm, but Bob's parents weren't interested. So he had his men sneak onto the land at night and smash the farm machinery; when he drove a herd of cattle through the farm and ruined all the crops, he won. Bob's parents couldn't take any more and they packed up and moved into Trouble.

Bob's mum and dad never recovered. They became ill and went to an early grave, but as their coffins were lowered into the ground, Bob swore that he wouldn't rest until he had got even with Horatio Ham.

Bob Ffrance Becomes An Outlaw

Young Bob wanted to stay with his friends in Trouble Town, but by now Ham had moved onto the Ffrance land, and had control of the river. He threatened to cut off the water supply if anyone in Trouble Town helped the young Ffrance boy.

Some of the townsfolk tried to

NOTICE

AnyOne CaUGHT HelpiNG YoUNG BoB FfrANCE WiLL bE SHoT!

By order of MArSHAL MCKAY

hide Bob, but when Ham made his vicious cousin, Mad Mickey McKay, the marshal of Trouble County, Bob knew he couldn't put his friends' lives at risk any more. One night he slipped out of his hiding place, and in an act of bravado, stole the marshal's horse and rode silently out of town.

'From then on,' said Bob, rolling out a blanket and throwing another over to me, 'I was an outlaw, wanted as a horse thief; anything I needed, I had to beg or borrow from the kind folk of Trouble, or steal from Horatio Ham and his cohorts.'

'But how did you survive, where did you grow up?' I asked.

'Oh, that's a long story, boy,' smiled Bob. 'Sometimes I lived on my own, sometimes with the Rapakwar Indians. They're good people and have as much cause to hate Horatio Ham as I have. He had a gang of hired gunfighters run them off their hunting grounds. Now they live way beyond the valley, waiting for the time when they can return home. Same as me. They taught me how to track and hunt and survive out in the open, as well as when to fight and when to run.'

This Horatio Ham sounds like a real twit!

'And where do you live now?'

'I live with a few others who have also been made outlaws by Horatio Ham, in a very secret hideout, and tomorrow I'll take you there. First we will have to get you a good, strong steed and that means going to Trouble; but all that can wait until morning.' With that, Wild Bob Ffrance pulled the blanket up under his chin and within a few seconds was snoring gently in sleep.

I Phone Home

I wish I could get to sleep as easily, but my head is full of cowboys and bandits, Indian braves and no-good varmints, so I've taken out my journal again. Will I find trouble in Trouble? Will I meet the horrible Horatio Ham and his cousin, Marshal Mad Mickey McKay and, if we get there, will Wild Bob Ffrance's gang of Desperados welcome me into their camp?

All of a sudden I felt further from home than ever, lying out under the vast night sky with just a snoring stranger for company, so I decided to give my mum a ring. I knew exactly what she would say; it was ages ago that a great bolt of lightning had hit my little raft and I had been swept down a mysterious tunnel into a vast jungle, but somehow for Mum it remains the very same day I started my adventures. Although she says the same thing every time I call her, the sound of her voice always makes me feel better. I picked up my mobile and called the number.

'Charlie? Is that you?' said Mum. 'Is everything all right?'

'Yes, Mum. I'm camping out with a notorious outlaw in the middle of the Wild West!'

'Sounds wonderful, dear,' she replied. 'Oh, wait a minute, Charlie. Here's your dad just come in. Now remember, don't be late for tea, and if you're passing the shops on the way back, please pick up a pint of milk. Bye.'

'Mum?' I called. But she had already hung up. Oh well, at least I know she's not worrying about me, even if I have been gone for years and years!

Now I've brought my journal up to date, I must get some sleep. Who knows what tomorrow may

bring? I'll write more just as soon as I can.
Goodnight, partners! Zzzzzzzzzz!

Riding Into Trouble

We woke up early the following morning and
after a quick cup of hot, bitter coffee, were
ready to go. Wild Bob Ffrance led his horse into
the clearing from where it had been tethered to
a tree for the night. Although Bob was dusty
and greasy, and his clothes were all tattered and
torn, Fortune, his magnificent black stallion,
gleamed like a piece of jet. Bob put a dirty boot
into a shining stirrup, swung a leg over the
stallion's back and then leaned over and lifted
me up onto the saddle behind him.

'Let's go and get you a horse,' he said, and
nudged Fortune into an easy trot.

We rode across the wide expanse of a dry and
dusty valley. This valley, according to Wild Bob,
had once been a fertile place full of trees and
long grasses. Then Horatio Ham had dammed
the river that fed it and now the whole area had
become a dust bowl. The watering holes had
long dried up; great cracks ran across the

parched ground and
bare tree stumps stood
where lush and leafy
glades had once grown.
Again, another
poor farmer had
been forced off
his land.

'It's like that all over the state,' said Wild Bob.
'Everywhere you go, Horatio Ham is taking
over. But he'll get what's comin' to him. It ain't
for nothin' that we've become known as the
Daredevil Desperados of Destiny.' And Bob
patted one of the six-guns that hung from his
belt.

Eventually we came to a high escarpment and
looked down on a bustling town of clapboard
houses, shops and inns.

'That's Trouble for you,' said Bob. 'I think
we'll go in the back way. Most of the townsfolk
are friendly – they hate Ham as much as I do –
but he's got spies everywhere. We don't want to
bump into one of them before we have to.' And
he urged his horse forward, taking a rough track
that led behind the buildings that lined Trouble's
Main Street.

We stopped at a large pen fenced with rough poles. It was called a corral and held about twenty beautiful horses. On one side of the pen was a large wooden stable. Wild Bob dismounted and tethered his horse.

'Come on, Kid,' he said and I jumped down and followed him as he quietly entered the stableblock through a back door. Bob crept noiselessly towards the front of the stables where large, double doors were open on to the main street. Here a small, stocky man was grooming a very small and stocky pony, whistling to himself.

There was a slight click as Bob cocked his gun.

'Don't you know any other tunes, you no-good varmint?' he asked from the shadows, and the groom froze with one hand on the pony's back. He slowly turned to face us and I don't know how he did it, but a gun had appeared in his hand, its dull sheen glinting in the subdued light.

'Come out of the shadows,' he ordered. 'Come out real slow, or I'll blow you to kingdom come.'

No, I thought. This can't be happening. I had

only been in town a couple of minutes and I was already involved in a gunfight!

'Don't,' I started to say, but Bob stepped out of the shadows, his gun still raised, and said, 'Not bad for an old-timer!'

The man stared into the gloom. 'Well, well, well,' he said, with a sly smile. 'If it ain't Wild Bob Ffrance, Daredevil Desperado and arch enemy of Trouble's noble benefactor, the honourable Horatio Ham.' And with that he spun his gun back into his holster and smiled. 'Where've you been the last few months, Bob?' And the two men stepped forward and embraced each other in a big bear-like hug. 'We thought maybe you'd been taken!'

Freecloud

'Wild Bob, taken by that lump of lard, Ham? That'll be the day!' said Bob with a wide grin on his face. 'It's good to see you, Cody,' he continued. 'I need a mount for my young partner here, the Lariat Kid.'

I blushed at my new nickname, feeling slightly foolish, but I have to admit it made me feel pretty good too!

26

'No problem, you know that, Bob,' replied Cody. He was a bony, white-haired old man, with a chin full of wiry whiskers and a mouth that contained just three teeth. 'Everyone in this god-forsaken town is behind you. Just take your pick; we've got some real good stock out back.'

'Yeah, I saw them,' said Bob. 'But what about the one you're sprucing up right now, Cody? He looks about the right size.'

Cody's whiskery jaw dropped. 'Oh boy, that would be beautiful,' he chuckled. 'This here pony is a birthday present from Ham to his son, and they're due in town any minute to pick it up!'

'Couldn't be sweeter,' said Bob, laughing.

'You'll have to tie me up, though, Bob. Make it look like a robbery, or Ham will have my guts for braces.'

'No problem,' Bob agreed, then turning to me he said, 'Say hello to your new best friend, Kid. What's her name, Cody?'

'Freecloud,' he answered. 'She's called Freecloud.'

She was certainly a beautiful pony, quiet and strong and a wonderful caramel colour, but she was also very small. She wasn't much bigger than a Shetland pony!

Freecloud

'She's a bit small, isn't she?' I said. 'I don't want to look daft!' And Freecloud snorted and looked at me as if to say, *daft am I? We'll soon see about that!*

'She's small but she's mighty fast,' said Cody. 'Take it from a man who knows horses,' Wild

Bob said. 'If she wasn't a bit special, there's no way that Ham would buy her for his son.'

But there were other things bothering me about my new 'gift'.

1) I didn't know how to ride a horse. Mechanical rhinos yes, horses no!

You can read about that in my Journal Gorilla City.

2) Freecloud wasn't Cody's horse to give away. Did I really want to annoy Horatio Ham, nasty land-grabbing tyrant or not, before I'd even met him?

Wild Bob must have guessed what I was thinking. 'Don't worry what Ham will think, Kid,' he said. 'You're in trouble just knowing me, and it's the duty of every Desperado to annoy, incense, railroad and disrupt Horatio Ham's existence in any and every way possible. You are on our side, aren't you, Kid?'

I didn't really have any choice, did I?

'Yeah, sure.' I sighed. 'Freecloud it is!'

How Not To Get On A Horse

After Cody had saddled Freecloud, Wild Bob tied and gagged the old-timer to make it look as if there had been a robbery. Then he brought Fortune through to the front of the store and mounted him. I watched very closely, but it looked simple enough. So, copying Wild Bob, I put my foot in a stirrup, pulled myself up with the saddle and swung my free leg over Freecloud's back.

Yikes, I thought, Freecloud's head has come off! But as I leaned forwards and cautiously looked down, I saw her tail, swishing patiently from side to side. How embarrassing, I had mounted my horse the wrong way round and ended up facing her bottom!

'*Wumpf mff!*' I could hear Cody sniggering from behind his gag, and I felt my face blush.

'C'mon, Kid,' said Bob sternly. 'This is no time to mess around.'

'Sorry,' I said, and I slipped down from Freecloud and remounted – again facing her bottom. How was that? I'm sure I did everything right.

'Wumpf mff munm!'

'All right, so I don't know how to ride a horse,' I cried. 'It's not that funny. We don't ride horses where I come from!'

'Did you hear that, Cody?' gasped Bob in astonishment. Cody's bony shoulders were shaking with laughter and tears were running down his face, and that got Wild Bob laughing too. 'What *do* you ride where you come from, then?' he sniggered.

'Rhinos mainly,' I said nonchalantly, remembering my long trek across the jungle plain on the back of Jakeman's marvellous mechanical rhino. 'I know how to ride rhinos!'

'What's a rhino when it's at home? Some special sort of horse that walks backwards?' said Bob. 'Oh, never mind. Let's get going; you'll just have to pick it up as you go along. So long, Cody, and thanks for all your help.' And he gave Fortune a nudge with his heels and moved off down the street.

A Quick And Painful Riding Lesson

Still blushing, I tried to swivel around in my saddle, but before I could, Freecloud had jogged out of the barn after Fortune. I leaned forward, flattening myself against Freecloud's back and stretched my arms as far around her fat tummy as they would go.

'Stop, Freecloud. STOP!' I begged, holding on for dear life.

All of a sudden, and I'm sure out of sheer vindictiveness, Freecloud broke into a fast trot.

'Help!' I yelled as I passed Wild Bob, still facing the wrong way. 'I don't know how to stop. *Ooof, ooof, ooof, ooof!*' I bounced wildly up and down on Freecloud's back, as if I was riding a bike down a steep flight of steps.

Now the townsfolk had started gathering around to join in the fun, pointing and laughing.

'Look,' someone cried. 'The circus has come to town!' This was so embarrassing; to think that I had once wrestled a giant river crocodile and now I was being made a fool of by a preposterous mini-pony with attitude! Oh, if only I had one of Jakeman's marvellous inventions to ride instead.

During my many adventures, one of Jakeman's inventions has always turned up, just in the nick of time. I don't know why and I don't even know who Jakeman is, but his magnificent mechanical rhino, his jet-powered swordfish and his super submawhale had helped me out of some very sticky situations. Why couldn't I have found a Jakeman's automated horse to ride – something that would do as it was told!

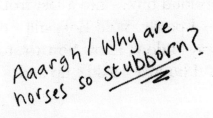

Aaargh! Why are horses so stubborn?

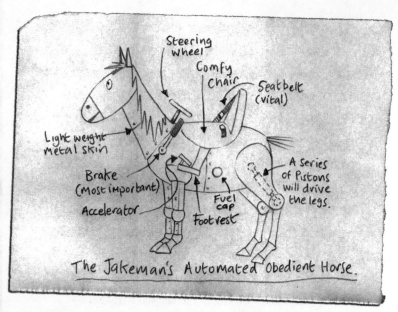

The Jakeman's Automated Obedient Horse.

(Here is my idea of what a Jakeman's Horse might look like!)

All of a sudden, Wild Bob was beside me. He grabbed Freecloud's reins and pulled us to a stop. Immediately, Freecloud kicked up her hind legs and I went sailing over her head, landing with a thump on the ground. The crowd roared with delight.

'Don't worry, Kid,' said Wild Bob with a grin. 'You've got to show her who's boss.' And at that moment Freecloud tossed her head, snorted, and looked me straight in the eye defiantly.

'Now try mounting her using your other foot,' Bob suggested. And do you know what – it worked! I found myself perched on Freecloud's back and pointing in the right direction.

'Brilliant!' I cried. 'Now, how do you steer and how do you stop?'

'Just pull on the reins,' said Bob. 'Left to go left; right to go right, and both together to stop. It's easy.' But as Freecloud tossed her head and stamped her hooves, I wasn't so sure that was true!

'Hadn't we better get going, before Horatio Ham finds out what we've done?' I asked. I really didn't want to bump into him while sitting on his son's new pony.

'All in good time, Kid. I need to get some supplies first,' said Bob with a grin. 'Anyway, Ham will already know all about us. He's got spies everywhere. So we may as well stick around and have some fun!'

Fun? What sort of fun? I didn't like the sound of this. I just wanted to get out of Trouble and ride far away – but it seemed Bob was determined to hang around until Ham showed up.

What on earth was going to happen then?

Horatio Ham

We carried on down Main Street, my eyes nervously scanning the crowds for someone who might possibly be Horatio Ham. But everyone appeared to know Wild Bob and was very friendly.

At the general store, Bob stopped and dismounted. 'We need some supplies,' he said. 'Come and lend a hand.' I pulled on the reins to stop Freecloud, but she tossed her head and took no notice. Much to everyone's amusement, I continued on down the road. Not again!

I pulled and pulled, but still nothing happened. Where's a brake handle when you need one? I heard Bob tut as he loped down the street after me and took the reins.

'You're really showing her who's boss,' he said with his silly grin as he led me back to the storefront.

As we entered the shop door, I caught a glimpse of a suspicious and scruffy-looking cowboy from the corner of my eye. He was sneaking hurriedly off towards the large saloon that stood on the far side of a square at the end of the street.

'Bob . . .' I started to say, but without even looking around, Bob smiled and said, 'I know.'

Inside the dark shop, the owner greeted Wild Bob as a friend. Bob picked up a large sack of flour and a brand-new lasso, which he handed to me. 'A brand-new lariat for the Lariat Kid,' he smiled and went to the counter to pay; but the shopkeeper refused to take his money.

'No way, Bob,' he said. 'You're a true friend to this town and we admire what you're doing against Ham. You've heard the latest, have you?'

'What might that be?' asked Bob, putting the fold of notes back in his pocket.

The Scorekeeper

'Horatio Ham has made himself President of Trouble Bank,' said the shopkeeper. 'Now he won't let us have our savings. He's got big plans for the town, says he. He needs the money more than we do, says he. It ain't fair! He's already built himself a brand-new ranch house. It's like a palace – indoor thunderbox and everything!'

'Is that so?' said Bob, going very quiet. 'Well, we'll have to see what we can do about that, won't we?'

'Good old Bob,' said the man, smiling widely behind his huge moustache. 'I knew we could depend on you.'

'So you can, friend,' said Bob. 'But first I have to get this stuff back to camp.' With that, Bob swung the bag of goods onto his shoulder and we walked out into the sunshine . . . and straight into a welcoming party of men, bristling with rifles.

'Good morning, Wild Bob Ffrance,' said a deep, gravelly voice from the centre of the group, and I knew who it was straight away: Horatio Ham. He was very tall and rather fat, with a fancy waistcoat stretched across his big, barrel-shaped belly. His eyes were tiny black slits that peered from the deep folds of his chubby cheeks, and he was staring at us with an arrogant sneer. He looked a thoroughly nasty piece of work.

'Aren't you going to introduce me to your new friend?' Ham asked, and with every

Horatio

Ham

movement he made, little waves of flesh
rippled across the greasy expanse of his face.
'I do so hate to arrest someone I haven't been
introduced to!'

Gunfight At Trouble Town

'Well, if it isn't the honourable Horatio Ham,' Bob replied, ignoring his question. 'I thought I might bump into you. Out for a walk with your bunch of bully boys?'

'I came to pick up a birthday present for my boy, Silas,' said Ham, and I noticed a large and bulky boy of about my own age, sticking his tongue out at me from behind his father's coat tails. 'I chose a nice little pony for him, but when I got to the stables I was told that someone had already taken it. You wouldn't happen to know anything about that, would you, Ffrance?'

Silas Ham.

'Sure,' said Wild Bob pushing his hat to the back of his head. 'We saw the horse, and the Kid here thought it was just the ride for him. The stable boss said it was for you, but as we're such old friends I didn't think you'd mind if I took it instead. You don't mind, do you, Ham?'

Horatio Ham's face darkened and his cheeks quivered with anger. Hold on! I thought. Don't get me involved – I didn't want to take the horse. But I knew I was already involved; I was standing next to Wild Bob Ffrance and that was enough to condemn me.

'Did you pay for the horse?' asked Ham through gritted teeth. Wild Bob didn't answer. 'Did you pay for those goods you're carrying now?' Again Wild Bob said nothing, while readjusting the heavy sack on his shoulder.

'Get ready to run, Kid,' he whispered from the side of his mouth. 'Run straight for your horse and ride like the wind.' *I can't ride a blooming horse*, I wanted to remind him, but I knew it wasn't the time or the place. Things were very serious indeed and I couldn't see a way out.

'So, you *haven't* paid. I thought as much,' said Ham with a smirk. 'Now you are a horse-thief twice over. It will be my pleasure to add the crime of shoplifting to your long list of misdemeanors. I'll take you over to the jail myself, right now.' As Horatio Ham started to take his gun from its holster, the group of men cocked their rifles and my knees started to knock. Wild Bob let the heavy sack fall from his shoulder and in one movement swung it up into the air. Everyone's eyes followed it as it sailed high over Ham's head.

As if by magic a gun appeared in Wild Bob's hand and he fired. *Bang! Bang! Bang!* The bullets ripped into the sack which exploded in a thick cloud of flour, filling the air around the gunmen's heads, clogging their eyes and ears and noses, and they doubled over in fits of coughing and swearing and sneezes.

'Time to go!' said Bob, and we raced down the sidewalk towards our horses. With the gorilla skills I'd learned in the jungle, it was no problem to leapfrog over the rail and land on Freecloud's back. For once she behaved herself, and with a kick I galloped down Main Street after Bob's stallion, with my eyes half-closed and holding onto Freecloud for dear life.

By the time Ham and his men had cleared

their eyes and lifted their rifles to their shoulders, we had rounded the corner and were racing out of town.

'Keep going, Kid,' yelled Bob. 'It won't be long before they're after us. Yee-hah!'

Sure enough, it was only a matter of a minute or two before I could hear the thundering of hooves behind us.

Help, how did I get into this mess!

The Lariat Kid

A deadly wasp!

Freecloud was small and fast and strong, but the horses after us were bigger and faster and stronger, and it wasn't long before red-hot bullets were whizzing round my ears like swarms of deadly wasps. Ham and his men were gaining on me every second.

I galloped along in a thick cloud of dust thrown up by Wild Bob's stallion. It made me cough and splutter and spit, but it was only this dust cloud that saved me from the chasing posse, making us all but invisible as they fired blindly into the fog of dirt. I could hear them getting nearer and nearer.

Then through the dirt cloud I saw Wild Bob gesturing towards a small track leading off to the right. As we reached it, Bob turned his horse without breaking stride, and – help! – how do you steer a horse again? I pulled on the reins, this way and that way, but it was too late. I went thundering straight past the turn, bouncing about in the saddle like a sack of potatoes.

Yikes! What was I going to do now? I yanked on the reins, Freecloud screeched to a halt and once again I went sailing over her head and crashed to the ground, my new lariat landing on top of me. With a whinny, Freecloud galloped away down the track after Fortune and Wild Bob.

'Freecloud, come back you stubborn old nag,' I cried chasing her down the track a little way.

I could hear Ham's posse getting closer every second; soon they would be on top of me. What could I do? I had to think fast. What would the Lariat Kid do? I sat up and as the rope slipped to the ground, an idea popped into my mind. I leaped to my feet and, finding the loop of the lasso, threw it over the stump

of a nearby tree. Quickly I ran across the track,
unravelling the lasso all the way. Finding a tall
standing stone on the other side of the track, I
looped the rope around it and dived to the
ground just as the posse came charging into
sight.

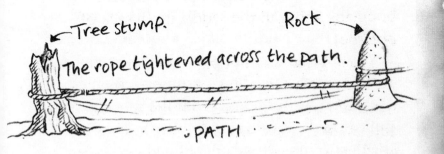

Tree stump.

Rock

The rope tightened across the path.

PATH

'Off to the right,' Horatio Ham was yelling.
'They turned up that track; can't you see the
dust trail?' The posse turned onto the track and
as they rode level with me, I pulled on the rope.
It leaped from the dust, tightening across the
path a few feet from the ground. Ham saw it
too late and his horse galloped straight into the
trap, tripping and stumbling and throwing Ham
from its back. The rest of the riders ploughed
into the back of his horse, and as their mounts
reared and kicked and whinnied, they fell to the

ground, dropping their rifles in the pandemonium. Ham landed with a sickening thump on the ground, the pistol in his holster went off with a crack and he yelled to one of his men.

'Yow! Take me home, Virgil, I think I've just shot myself in the foot!'

As the men flailed around on the ground, rubbing their painful rears and holding bruised arms, Wild Bob Ffrance came thundering back down the track, leading a grumpy-looking Freecloud by her reins. From the way she pulled on the bridle and dug her hooves into the dusty path, I think she hoped she'd seen the last of me.

'That's some mighty fine lasso work, Kid,' Bob smiled, hauling me onto the pony by the scruff of my neck. 'That should teach you,' he added to Ham. 'Don't ever mess with the Lariat Kid!' And with a slap to the rear of my irritated pony and a 'Yee-hah!' we galloped away down the track again, followed by a couple of half-hearted shots from Ham's posse.

~~Destiny~~ Destination Destiny

We rode at full gallop for another half-hour, along dry riverbeds, through isolated groves of cactus trees and across a wide and empty plain towards a range of low mountains. All of a sudden a huge shadow passed over the ground in front of us, and for a moment the air turned chilly. I shivered and looked up into the sky, and caught a glimpse of a large black shape disappearing into a bank of clouds.

'What was that?' I asked.

'Mapwai,' muttered Wild Bob with a shudder, staring up into the now empty sky with wide, fearful eyes. This was the first time I had seen the outlaw look scared.

'What's Mapwai?' I asked.

'With any luck, Kid, you'll never have to find out,' said Bob seriously. 'C'mon, we've still got a little way to go.'

As we grew nearer, I could see that one of the mountains was perfectly conical in shape, its summit chopped flat and emitting large puffs of smoke. It's a volcano, I thought. A volcano that looked as if it might erupt at any minute; what on earth were we heading towards that for?

'There she is,' said Wild Bob, pointing at the funnel-shaped flame-thrower of a mountain. 'That's home. That's Destiny Mountain!'

DESTINY!

Oh, brilliant, I thought. Things just keep on getting better and better!

We rode straight towards the volcano. When we reached the base I thought Bob was going to try and ride straight up the sheer sides, but at the last minute he turned his horse and we trotted through the scrub that grew around the base of the mountain. Gradually the bushes started to get thicker and thicker, and Bob turned this way and that, following an invisible path through them.

Then, once again, the side of the mountain rose before us like a huge wall. It seemed we could go no further, but Bob turned back on himself and followed the side of the mountain for a bit, before disappearing into thin air!

Entering Destiny

One minute he was there and the next he was gone. I was alone in the bush, staring at the empty space he had just occupied. My jaw dropped open in amazement, and for a minute I sat there on Freecloud's back like a complete lemon, looking this way and that. Midges buzzed in the warm air and somewhere I could hear the sound of a waterfall, but everything else was quiet. I couldn't hear the clop of Bob's horse, or the thin whistling that he constantly made between his teeth as he rode. I was alone. I was lost. I was . . .

'Are you coming, or are you just going to sit there for the rest of the day?' asked Bob, and once again I stared in wonder, for all I could see was his head. It seemed to float in mid-air about four metres up the side of the mountain. Then his stallion's head appeared, followed by its neck, and I began to understand exactly what I was seeing.

There was a separate wall of rock that followed the curve of the mountainside about a metre and a half in front of the mountain itself, and it so completely matched the colour and texture of the volcano as to be almost invisible. As I nudged Freecloud forwards, I came to the spot where Bob had disappeared and saw a narrow entrance to a path that led up the side of the volcano, completely shielded from view by the solid wall of rock on the other side.

'Pretty sweet, eh?' said Bob, smiling widely.

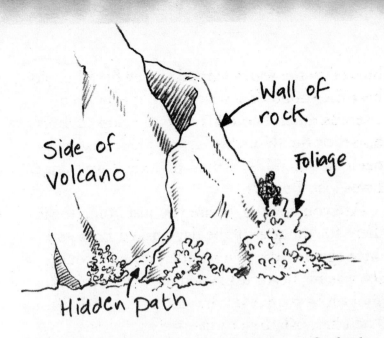

Side of volcano

Wall of rock

Foliage

Hidden path

'It'll be pure bad luck if anybody ever finds the entrance to Destiny.' He kicked his horse and I followed him up the rocky pathway. Every now and then, there was a small gap in the outside wall and, looking out, I could see we had risen hundreds of metres above the surrounding plain. It was a wonderful view and a fantastic lookout post. You would be able to see any enemies for miles. So it seemed strange that there wasn't a lookout. If anyone did find the hidden path, it seemed that they could walk straight into the Desperados' camp.

Then I heard a whistle, surprisingly close by, and it was answered by the hoot of an owl and

I realized we had been watched all the way. The path entered the large archway of a tunnel in the mountainside, and looking up, I saw holes in the tunnel roof, like the murder holes in a castle gateway. If we had been enemies I am sure that we would have been showered with all manner of rocks and boulders.

Suddenly we were through the tunnel, emerging into the bright sunlight on a platform of rock that looked down into the interior of the volcano. What a wonderful sight it was!

The sides of the volcano were sheer and high and completely hollow. Large hawks soared over the circle of sky above our heads; on all sides water cascaded down, forming deep green pools amongst the rocks at the base of the cliff face. The floor of the volcano was covered in lush grass on which the horses could feed, and near the centre were a group of rickety wooden huts, from where a group of men looked up at our approach. I began to feel very nervous as we trotted down into the interior of the volcano to meet them.

The Desperados

Almost immediately we were surrounded by a gang of the most disreputable looking characters I'd seen since escaping from the grisly lady pirates. They were dirty, smelly and armed to the teeth with an amazing assortment of guns and rifles and daggers. One of them even had his pockets stuffed full with sticks of dynamite. If he tripped over we would have all been blown to kingdom come. So, these were the famous Daredevil Desperados! They looked fierce and unfriendly, and they all started talking at once.

'Everything go OK, Bob?'

'Who's your prisoner, Bob?'

'Are we going to torture him straight away, or wait until after dinner?'

'Whoa! Hold your horses, boys. This here is the Lariat Kid, and he's not a prisoner, he's a friend, a good friend. We really had some fun hounding Horatio Ham. Cornelius, if dinner is ready, serve it up and I'll tell you all about it.'

As we sat around the campfire, eating generous portions of bacon and beans (don't cowboys eat anything else?) and drinking glasses of something called Red-eye, Wild Bob told them all about how I had rolled into his camp, and how I had swiped Ham Junior's horse, and how I brought down the whole of Ham's posse with one flick of my lasso! The Desperados were delighted.

'Oh, real sweet, I wish I'd seen that,' said one of the gang, snorting down his nose. His shoulders were shaking with mirth, but his face stayed as long as a wet Sunday. 'My name's Sneaky Pete. Glad to make your acquaintance, Kid.' And with that, all the Desperados started to introduce themselves, welcoming me as one of their own. All except one man who sat slightly apart from the group and just sat watching me, making me feel very uneasy.

'That's Gentleman Jim, a real pistolero,' said Sneaky, pointing over at him. 'He's Wild Bob's number two. He don't say much, but he's OK . . . as long as you don't cross him.'

We had a fine old feast; the beans and the Red-eye flowed

The Desperados loved this drink.

RED-EYE OLD GUTROT

freely and the Desperados danced and sang, stamping their boots in the dust as Sneaky Pete played a battered old banjo. *Yee-hah!* This is the song that they sang:

When Ham rode into town, the wind howled just like a hound,
Lightning split the heavens and thunder shook the ground,
Daytime turned as black as night and clocks stopped on the shelf,
When Ham rode into Trouble, we thought it was the hound of hell himself.

Horatio Ham is a devil of a man, he'll take just what he wants then say goodbye,
Horatio Ham is the devil's own man, he'll stake you out in the noonday sun and leave you there to fry.

When Ham takes a walk down Main Street, flowers shrivel up and die,
The ground begins to tremble and children start to cry,
But when Wild Bob catches up with him, he'll know he's met his match,
Because Ham will need the doctor, but Bob won't bear a scratch.

*Horatio Ham is the devil of a man, he'll take just
what he wants then say goodbye,
Horatio Ham is the devil's own man, he's sold his very
soul and now he is bound to die.*

My New Pals

Keeping to my promise to record all the strange
and wonderful people and creatures I meet, here
are a few sketches of my new friends. And what a
lovely bunch of vagabonds they are!

Wild Bob Ffrance
Wild Bob is leader of the
Daredevil Desperados.
You've already met him
and know him for
the amiable, brave
and reckless hero
of the people
that he is.

Sneaky
Pete was
always jolly!

Sneaky Pete

Poor old Sneaky is blessed with the most
miserable face I've ever seen. It's a real shame
because he is really very cheerful and always
ready with a joke. No one has ever seen Sneaky
Pete smile; if something amuses him he just
gives a loud snort through his nose. He is the
gang's intelligence gatherer.

Gentleman
Jim Silver
Gunfighter

Gentleman Jim Silver

Gentleman Jim is a real dandy and dresses in black from head to toe. He has pure white hair and wears a hat pulled down low to protect his pale pink eyes. His boots sport sparkling rhinestones and silver spurs and he wears two silver revolvers with pearl handles. He is a quiet thinker, a slow talker, and a very dangerous gunslinger. Of all the Desperados, I find Gentleman Jim by far the scariest.

Mick the Miner

A giant of a man and the hairiest thing on two legs I've seen since meeting Thrak, King of the Gorillas. He is an expert at digging tunnels, and is able to take a full-grown man in each hand and lift them clean off the ground. Whatever you do, don't get into a wrestling match with Mick the Miner; he will make mincemeat of you!

Mick the Miner is so hairy, he looks just like a scribble!

Jake 'Pint-pot' Penley

A fierce and tiny powerhouse of a Desperado, with just one eye and one leg. Rumour has it that his wooden leg has been specially adapted to help him fight, and he has to be seen to be believed! I don't know if this is true.

Now it's late in the evening and everything is quiet except for the call of the coyotes in the distance. I'm plum-tuckered out after my day's amazing adventures. Not surprising, really; I've made friends with a bunch of outlaws, outwitted the most powerful man in the territory and stolen his son's horse. (Though if I'd known then what I know now about Freecloud, Silas Ham could have kept the bad-tempered, disobedient, grumpy, good-for-nothing brute!)

I have been given a berth in a small bunkhouse, which consists of four bunks, a locker for each man, a stove and a small table and some chairs. It's nice and snug, and now I've finished bringing my journal up to date, I must get some sleep. Goodnight, partners!

Three Hours Later

Boy, do these Desperados snore. What's more, with the after-effects of so many baked beans, that's not all they do; I've been woken up three times already, thinking that the volcano was erupting!

Phwar!

Pooee!

Joining The Desperados!

The next morning after a long breakfast (bacon and beans!) and a very, very quick wash under a freezing cold waterfall, Wild Bob made an announcement.

'Now listen, partners,' he said. 'The Lariat Kid has saved my life once and upset Horatio

Ham twice. So, I propose we make him a full member of the Daredevil Desperados. What do you say, boys?'

'Sure thing, boss. Yee-hah!' cried the gang, cheering and slapping me good-naturedly on the back while firing their guns in the air. All except Gentleman Jim Silver, who stood a little way off, staring at me from the deep shadow cast by the brim of his black hat.

'What do you say, Jim?' asked Wild Bob.

'We don't have much choice, do we?' he said in a slow and lazy voice. 'Now he knows the whereabouts of Destiny. Because we all know what happens to outsiders who know where our hideout is, don't we?'

Nobody explained *what* happened to unwelcome visitors to Destiny, and I didn't really want to find out, so I was mighty glad to become a fully-fledged fugitive and swear the oath of allegiance to the Daredevil Desperados of Destiny.

The Oath of Allegiance to The Daredevil Desperados Of Destiny

I swear to uphold the ideals of
The Daredevil Desperados Of Destiny,
which are:

1) To make Horatio Ham's life a misery

2) To hound and harass Horatio Ham
at every turn

3) To make Horatio Ham look stupid in
front of everybody (not difficult!)

4) To defend any citizen against
Horatio Ham's nefarious (that means
wicked) activities

5) To remain a Daredevil Desperado
until Horatio Ham has been defeated

6) To keep the whereabouts of Destiny
a secret *Wild Bob france*

P.S. 7) To never complain about Cornelius Duff's
unchanging menu of bacon and beans!

Then I was taught the Desperados' secret handshake. It is done with the left hand in order to keep your shooting hand ready to draw at the first sign of trouble. This is the handshake, but please remember it is TOP SECRET and I will be in real trouble if any of the others find out I've written it down in here:

I did find out, when I was sneaking a look at this strange diary you're always writing in. I've crossed out your drawing of our secret handshake before any harm has been done, so we'll say no more about it. Wild Bob

It was a real honour to become a lifelong Daredevil Desperado, but somehow I will have to tell them that I need to be moving on as soon as possible; I really must continue my journey home, but now that I'm a life member, will they let me leave?

At lunchtime, as I sat by the campfire, I told my new pals about my incredible journey. I told them everything: about leaving home and getting washed away on my raft; about the crocodile and the jungle; Thrak; the Perfumed Pirates and finally the evil Puppet Master.

I didn't think they would believe me, but the outlaws were amazed by my adventures and said I was the bravest Desperado of them all. They promised to try and help me get back home if they could – just as soon as I had helped them defeat Horatio Ham!

Oh well, it looks like I've got a job to do before I can think about going home. I will have to prepare myself for the task and practise lassoing until I'm as good as everyone thinks I am! First, though, I really want to speak to my mum. Even if she does say exactly the same thing every time, it lets me know that everything is still all right at home. I wound up my phone charger and tapped in my home number on the mobile.

'Mum!' I said when I heard her voice.

'Charlie? Is that you? Is everything all right?'

'Yes, Mum. I'm safe . . . I've joined a gang of Desperate Desperados and I have to stay here until we've defeated a baddy called Horatio Ham!'

'Sounds wonderful, dear,' she replied. 'Just get home soon, Charlie. You're very late and your dinner's quite cold.'

'Mum?' I called, suddenly very worried. Surely that's not what she usually said. Has something happened; has something changed? 'Mum?' I cried again, but she had already hung up. I tried ringing back, but I couldn't get a signal. I hope everything is all right – but the sooner I get home, the better . . .

Later That Day

Wild Bob said he was going to be in a meeting most of the afternoon, planning the Desperados' next move against Horatio Ham.

'You'll have to amuse yourself for a bit,' he said. 'But be careful; we sometimes get the odd mountain bear or cougar wandering into camp, and they can be a bit of a handful.'

I didn't mind being left to my own devices. I knew what I wanted to do. I had watched Yellow

How to twirl your lasso and turn your wrist over at the same time.

Bill, one of the Desperados, practising with his lasso, and I noticed how he turned his wrist over as he twirled the loop above his head.

Well, it looks easy enough, I thought, and I went to practise with my own lasso, well out of the way of the others. I didn't want anyone to see that I wasn't quite as good as Wild Bob had led them to believe!

I spent most of the afternoon trying to get the rope flying through the air and landing on a target and, oh boy, it isn't easy. I think I lassoed myself a hundred times, and an innocent lizard once, before I somehow got the rope in a hopeless tangle and spent an hour untying all the knots! I'm never going to get the hang of this. Though at the end of the day, I did manage to lasso a stone about a metre in front of me. That's real progress!

The Following Day

More beans.

Practice riding Freecloud. She's still very disobedient, but I'm getting the hang of it.

More practice with my lasso. (I need it!)

Another singsong around the campfire (with bean supper).

The Next Day

Beans, followed by terrible tummy ache.

More practice on Freecloud. I think we know who the boss is now – *she* is, and since I've accepted that, things have been much better!

More practice with my lasso – getting better.

Multiple bottom explosions – tummy ache gone!

The Day After That

I carried on practising my lariat skills. I am not doing too badly; all my experience of swinging on vines through Gorilla City and climbing the rigging on the *Betty Mae* has given me a feel for handling ropes and I soon had the lariat plopping onto the little rocks that I used as targets.

As I practised, I noticed some really bizarre creatures living amongst the rocks, and although I am now a Desperado I'm still first and foremost an intrepid explorer, so I have jotted down a description of a couple of the weirdest animals and named them:

The Slam Dunk Toad

A harmless and comical creature, the Slam Dunk Toad can really make you jump as its flat, fat body lands with a loud slap on a rock right next to you!

SPLAT!

The Slam Dunk Toad.

The Galleon Lizard

The Galleon
Lizard's
body is the
shape of a
fat-hulled
galleon,
and its back
is crested
with spines and
fans, like sails
and rigging.
Don't be fooled
if you see one
lazily
basking in
the sun on
a rock; they can move very quickly and their
spines are deadly poisonous.

The Galleon Lizard

Staring Disaster In The Face!

HELP!

Please excuse my wobbly handwriting, but my hands are still shaking with fear. It was nearly all over for me today. I didn't know a lasso could get you into so much danger. If it hadn't been for some double-quick thinking on my part and some real fancy shooting from Gentleman Jim Silver, I would be just a memory by now!

After my usual morning chow-down (I'm picking up the Desperado lingo quite quickly) and checking the Desperado Notice Board for any new instructions, I took my lariat across to the practice area. I stood some stones on a large rock, took a hundred paces back and started to spin the lasso over my head. Once, twice, and throw. The rope snaked through the air and landed over the stone I had been aiming for. I tried again and succeeded again.

Now I did the same, but this time on the move. I threw my lasso whilst running; I threw it as I span round from low down, left-handed, right-handed; I threw the lasso from the back of a galloping Freecloud, and every time I hit my chosen target. I was good; I finally felt I might deserve the nickname of the Lariat Kid.

Feeling pleased with myself, I was just heading back towards the huts when a slight movement among the rocks caught my eye, and instinctively I turned and threw the rope. I thought it was a plant waving in the breeze, but as the loop of my lariat dropped over it and I pulled hard to tighten it, I realized there wasn't even a breeze in the air. So what was making the plant wave?

I gave the rope a yank, trying to pull the object out of the rock.

It looked like a funny plant!

Nothing happened so I yanked again, hard. Suddenly, and with a terrifying roar, a huge cougar leaped on top of the rock and I saw what I had done – I had lassoed its tail, which had been sticking up above the top of the boulder. BIG MISTAKE!

Any Umbrellas?

Spitting and hissing, the cougar attacked, giving me little time to think. The animal launched itself at me with deadly claws extended and its huge fanged mouth open in a terrific and angry

74

roar. I did the first thing that came into my head; reaching over my shoulder, I pulled the extending umbrella from my rucksack. As the animal dived towards me, I  dropped to my knees, avoiding its razor-like talons, and thrust the umbrella into its gaping jaw while pressing the release button.

I just managed to roll away as the lion landed heavily on the ground and my umbrella snapped open, forcing its mouth wider still. The spokes of my brolly dug painfully into the roof of its mouth; now the animal couldn't bite, and in a mad frenzy the cougar ripped at the contraption, shredding the cover and pulverizing the wire frame. As I backed away trying to find a place to hide, the cougar spat out the remains of my umbrella, and with a satisfied look started to creep towards me.

Now what? I was all out of umbrellas; I was all out of Paterchak's mint humbugs and pirate cutlasses. I was all out of ideas! Then, as I stepped back against the volcano's sheer wall and realized I had nowhere to run, the ground in front of the cougar exploded in a puff of dust and the sound of a pistol shot echoed around the bowl of the volcano.

Time For A Trim

I looked across to where the shot had come from and there, of all people, stood Gentleman Jim Silver, his hat pulled low over his eyes and one of his pearl-handled pistols smoking in his right hand. The angry cougar took another step towards me, and again a bullet ripped into the ground in front of it. Now the massive beast turned and with a roar, charged at Silver, streaking across the ground in a blur of furious yellow fur. In an instant, Silver dipped his left hand, drawing his other pistol, and with his two guns spitting lead he sprayed the ground in front of the charging beast, forcing it to turn away. A final shot cut across the animal's rump, singed its fur and sent it racing for the rocks.

The animal leaped across the boulders and without stopping, climbed the cliff face higher and higher, finally disappearing into the mouth of a cave that appeared as a tiny black dot high in the volcano's wall.

'Close call,' drawled Gentleman Jim, and with a chuckle he turned and headed back to the huts. Incredible! The silent, stand-offish gunman had come to my rescue.

'Thanks!' I called after him. Gentleman Jim pointed towards the ground where the cougar had charged. 'You can keep them as a souvenir,' he said as he disappeared inside his bunkhouse.

Keep what? I thought, and hurried over to where he had pointed. There, lying in the dust, were eight long cougar claws that he had neatly trimmed with his superb shooting. Excellent! These will be undeniable proof of my terrible encounter with a cantankerous cougar. Wait until I show my friends back at school!

A couple of my cougar claws!

<u>Plans</u>

This evening we all sat down to our supper of
beans and bacon (I never thought I would say
this, but I'm getting a bit tired of the
Desperados' menu) and while we ate, Wild Bob
told us the plans for tomorrow. He chalked a
diagram of Trouble Town onto a painted
board, and explained how we were going to rob
Trouble Bank! I was appalled – surely we were
supposed to be helping the people of Trouble,
not taking their money!

'Calm down, partner,' said Wild Bob. 'You
heard what the storekeeper said. Ham has taken
over the bank and won't let the townsfolk have
their own money. We're not going to steal the
money, we're going to liberate it and give it
back to the people who own it. That should set
Ham's blood a-boiling!'

'Yee-hah!' cheered the Desperados.

'That's brilliant!' I cried. 'Just like Robin
Hood.'

'I said we weren't robbin' anybody,' said Wild
Bob. 'Now this ain't gonna be easy, so everyone
must be on their best form. I don't want to

have to go back for some straggler who's got themselves thrown in jail.' I don't know why, but I had the feeling that Wild Bob was looking at me when he said that!

Now I'm lying in bed, images of shootouts and chases flashing through my head as the sound of the Desperados' snores shake our flimsy wooden hut. I must try and get some sleep, though. Otherwise I will be too dozy to take part in tomorrow's raid. I will write more just as soon as I can.

The Following Day

OH NO! After all our planning and Wild Bob's warnings, I'm writing this part of my journal from inside Trouble County Jail! The only other prisoner is a young Indian brave, about my own age; but either he doesn't speak English, or he's not very friendly, because all he does is sit cross-legged on his bunk, silently staring into space.

Apparently I only have a few hours left, for at sunrise tomorrow Horatio Ham and Mad Marshal Mickey McKay have promised me a big surprise. I don't know what sort of surprise, but

I know it won't be nice; a while ago they got
Nathaniel Slaughter, the town undertaker, to
come and measure me for a coffin! Mad
McKay has put extra guards on the jailhouse,
but I do hope Wild Bob rescues me tonight.
In the meantime I'll tell you all about our bank
raid.

Six of us rode into town: Wild Bob; Gentleman
Jim; Sneaky Pete; Jake 'Pint-size' Penley, Yellow
Bill, who shook like a leaf at the first sign of
trouble but was really as brave as a lion; and
finally myself, the Lariat Kid.

Some of the other Desperados were waiting
outside town as extra cover, in case we had to
retreat, and the rest were back at Destiny
guarding the hideout. My heart was pounding
as we rode quietly down Main Street. I had
never robbed a bank before, and I knew that
Horatio Ham would not let us take the money
without a fight. But I had sworn to uphold the
Desperado creed and I was determined to do
my best.

It was early morning when we rode into Trouble Town.

The Lariat Kid Strikes

There were only a few early risers about and the town seemed calm and peaceful. There was no sign of Ham, but all of a sudden a lone cowboy spotted us and raced down the sidewalk.

'That's one of Ham's men. Take him, Kid,' said Wild Bob, and I unhooked my lariat and in one fluid movement had it spinning over my head; with a flick of the wrist I sent it arcing through the air, falling over the man's shoulders and slipping down to tighten around his ankles. I yanked and he came crashing down onto the wooden sidewalk. Brilliant, it worked! All my practising had paid off.

'That was real sweet, Kid,' said Wild Bob, and I beamed with pride.

Sneaky Pete ran over to the floored man. With a thin cord he tied the man's hands and feet and put a gag around his mouth. None of the townsfolk tried to stop us. They were firmly on our side, but they knew there might be trouble and started to head back home.

'Good morning, Bob,' said a lady in a bright crimson dress, smiling winningly. Her face was painted like a china doll's and she fluttered her long eyelashes. 'When are you going to come and see me, you big Daredevil Desperado, you?'

Bob's face blushed as red as the lady's dress.

'Well I . . . we're here on business. Excuse me, ma'am,' he stuttered.

'Who's that?' I asked as she winked at Bob and hurried away.

'Oh, er . . . local schoolmistress,' said Bob, and I heard Sneaky Pete give a loud snort. Schoolmistress! I thought. She's certainly not like any of the teachers at St Beckham's.

We carried on towards the bank where we loosely tied up our horses, ready for a quick getaway.

The Biggest Bullion Raid In Trouble's Troubled History - NOT!

'OK, this is it!' said Wild Bob in a serious voice, and I pulled my neckerchief over my face for a mask, as I'd seen cowboys do on the telly.

'There's no point in that, Kid,' smiled Gentleman Jim. 'Everyone knows who we are!'

'Is everybody ready?' asked Bob. 'Let's go. Victory to the Daredevil Desperados of Destiny!'

'Yee-hah!' we all shouted, and with Wild Bob leading, we crashed through the doors of the bank, Bob and Gentleman Jim firing their pistols into the ceiling for effect. My heart pounded with excitement and fear, but feeling more confident after the success with my lariat, I raced in . . . and promptly fell flat on my face!

'Mind the step,' said a lone voice from behind a long counter. I scrambled to my feet with as much dignity as I could muster.

'Nobody move. This is a hold-up!' yelled Wild Bob scanning the room with his pistol; but he needn't have bothered because the bank was empty. All except for the dusty old bank teller who had told me to mind my step, and was looking at us over his half-moon spectacles as calmly as though he dealt with bank robbers every working day.

'I'm sorry, Bob, you're too late; the money's already been stolen!' said the elderly man.

The old Bank Teller.

'Ham guessed you might be planning something like this and he took all the cash first thing this morning.' And the teller pointed to an iron safe at the back of the room. Its heavy door stood open and we could see he was telling the truth. The safe was as bare as old Mother Hubbard's cupboard.

'Where's he taken it?' asked Wild Bob.

'I've no idea, but wherever he is, he'll be laughing his socks off. He thinks he's got the better of you.'

'We'll soon see about that,' said Bob, his hackles rising. 'He won't make a monkey out of me. Come on, boys!' And Wild Bob turned on his heels and marched towards the door.

'Good luck, Bob, but watch out. Ham's got his men everywhere.'

I don't think so, I thought. We only saw one, and I caught him. We opened the bank's door
... AND
WALKED
STRAIGHT
INTO
A HAIL OF
GUNFIRE!

BANG!

CRACK!

PEEAW!

Mayhem In Main Street

'Down!' yelled Wild Bob, and we hit the deck and rolled behind any cover we could find. Bob and I crouched behind a wagon tied up outside. Gentleman Jim and Sneaky dived behind a stone water trough; Pint-pot and Yellow Bill had rolled back inside the bank and were at an open window, pistols at the ready.

'There they are,' said Wild Bob, pointing up at the rooftops opposite the bank. 'They must have been hiding there all the time, waiting for us to make our move.' The rest of the street was now deserted. Wild Bob poked his head around the side of the wagon, and another swarm of bullets ricocheted all around us, sending great splinters of wood flying through the air like deadly darts. Yikes, what had I got myself into?

A whistle sounded from Gentleman Jim

behind the water trough. He was pointing to a porch above the barber's, where three of Ham's men were crouched underneath its large painted sign. Wild Bob nodded, and as the gunfire lulled, both men rolled out into the open, crouched on one knee for an instant as they sent a spray of bullets zinging through the air, shooting away the brackets that held up the signboard. Then they continued their roll until they had changed places; Bob was now hidden behind the water trough and Gentleman Jim was with me behind the wagon.

At the same time, CRASH!, the signboard dropped from its brackets onto the heads of the hapless hard nuts below, knocking them clean out!

'Sweet,' I said and Gentleman Jim grinned. Then, 'Watch out!' I cried, as two men came running across the sloping roof outside the saddler's, guns cocked and ready to fire.

'They're mine,' called Sneaky Pete and he raised his buffalo rifle and fired. BOOM! The powerful rifle shot one of the supporting pillars clean away and the roof started to collapse.

BOOM!

'Aaargh!' the men cried as they slid down the disintegrating tiles. *Boof!* One man landed with a heavy thud on the ground below. *Splash!* The other fell head-first into a smelly waterbutt. They lay motionless, knocked cold, and Sneaky Pete snorted in amusement though his face was still as mournful as a sad-faced clown's.

A Tornado Of Bullets!

Ham's men started firing at once, and within seconds it was complete chaos. They crouched on every rooftop and behind every sign; their guns spitting lead and sending out orange tongues of fire.

We ducked our heads as the air filled with the roar of gunfire. We've had it! I thought as the wagon in front of us started to collapse under a hail of bullets. Surely we were beaten; there were just too many of them. Then, with a banshee yell, Pint-pot launched himself through the bank window.

'Cover me!' he called and stormed into the middle of the road. As the Desperados started up a barrage of their own, Pint-pot planted his wooden leg in the mud and with a kick, started to spin round like a top.

Jake 'Pint-pot' Penley springs into action!

Rrrratatatatatat! With the destructive power of a tornado, Pint-pot fired in a furious frenzy while spinning round and round; he was as fast as a machine gun, quickly pulling one pair of pistols after another from the belts across his chest. *Whizz! Ptang!* Bullets ricocheted off signboards and rooftops and chimney pots, and, overwhelmed by the ferocity of the attack and in complete panic, Ham's men threw down their weapons and scattered.

'Yeehah!' crowed Wild Bob, walking out to congratulate Pint-pot. It was then that I heard a noise and looking up saw one lone gunman crouched on the portico behind us. He must have worked his way round the back during the gunfight and was just about to bring his rifle up to aim at Wild Bob Ffrance. I didn't have time to think, but acted on instinct. I ran along the curb, unfurling my lariat at the same time. I span the rope, once, twice, and let it fly.

The lasso tightened around a beam protruding from the porch roof, and as I grabbed the rope tight, I kicked against the sidewalk and went soaring upwards. Grip and Grapple would have been proud of me; as the rifleman cocked his weapon, I swung up above

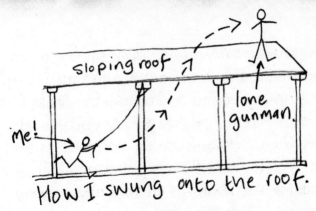

sloping roof

lone gunman.

me!

How I swung onto the roof.

the roof and let go. Sailing silently through the air – *CRASH!* – I landed on the man, knocking him and his rifle to the street below.

'Yippee-yi-oh!' I cried in relief, jumping down from the portico. My heart was racing and my hands were shaking, but the bank raid was over, and although we hadn't got any money, I was still in one piece!

'Well done, Lariat Kid!' said Wild Bob. 'Now let's get out of here.'

The Schoolmistress Comes To Our Aid

We rode out of town to meet up with the other Desperados, and as we approached the copse, I heard them cock their rifles.

'It's only us,' cried Wild Bob as we galloped amongst the trees.

'Everything OK, boss?' asked Mick the Miner. 'We heard plenty of shootin' and weren't sure whether to come and join in the fun!'

'Nothing we couldn't handle,' said Bob. 'But we haven't got the money. Ham's already taken it and we don't know where, darn it! He's made us look a right bunch of charlies, no offence, Kid. We've got to find out where he's taken it.'

Just then, I spotted a small dot on the horizon. 'Someone's coming,' I yelled, and immediately the Desperados drew their weapons.

'Who is it, Kid?' asked Bob.

'I'm not sure, just a minute,' I said, taking the telescope from my rucksack and training it on the approaching figure. 'It's that schoolmistress you were talking to. She's riding out in a little buggy.'

Soon the schoolmistress had steered her buggy into the copse and brought it to a halt.

'I thought I might find you here, Bob,' she said, fluttering her long eyelashes.

'What do you want, Susie?' asked Wild Bob, immediately starting to go red with embarassment.

'I bet you'd just love to know where Horatio Ham is, wouldn't you?' said Susie coyly, giving Bob the sweetest of smiles.

'Well, sure,' said Bob, getting a little flustered under her lingering gaze. 'Do you know where he is?'

'Oh, sure I do,' said Susie, lazily. 'But I can't give away information like that for nothing. Why, who knows what Ham would do if he ever found out I'd given him away.'

'Of course, Susie,' said Wild Bob, feeling in his pockets for some money. 'How much do you want?'

'Oh, I don't want money, Bob,' said Susie.

'You don't?' said Bob, gulping loudly.

'No Bob, I want a kiss. A long, lingering smacker of a kiss.'

'Yee-hah!' cried the rest of the Desperados. 'Go on, boss, give her a kiss!'

Bob went redder than ever and, closing his eyes, he leaned from his saddle to where Susie sat in her buggy, face raised and lips puckered.

Bob gave Susie the slightest of pecks but Susie's arm snaked around the back of his neck and pulled him onto her lips again.

They kissed . . . and kissed . . . and kissed (eugh!) and the Desperados cheered until, finally, Susie let Bob go. He didn't look quite such a wild Desperado anymore; he had a stunned look on his face and his mouth was smeared with lipstick.

'Now, that wasn't so bad, was it?' said Susie, with a smile.

'No,' croaked Wild Bob. 'Now, where's Horatio Ham?'

'You'll find him at the Pink Elephant Saloon, and he's got the money with him.'

'Sweet,' smiled Wild Bob, looking more himself all of a sudden. 'Well, boys, it looks like our trip might not be wasted after all. Thank you, Susie, you're a pal.'

'It was a pleasure,' said Susie. 'And you might need my help again. Ham thinks you've left town with your tail between your legs, even though you managed to scare off most of his men; now he's feeling safe, but he's still got one guard posted outside the saloon, who is armed to the teeth. I'm sure I can get rid of him quietly, if you want to take Ham by surprise.'

Bob sat thinking a while and then said, 'OK, Susie, if you're sure. Kid, you and Mick the Miner, come with me. The rest of you, position yourselves around the town and keep an eye out in case Ham's gunfighters return.'

Changing The Guard

Main Street was still deserted as Wild Bob, Mick the Miner and I followed the schoolmistress in her buggy. The rest of the Desperados fanned out to position themselves around town. As we approached the saloon, the three of us dismounted and led our horses up a narrow alleyway, where we watched as Susie stopped her buggy outside the saloon.

I could see her whispering something to the guard who was armed with an array of pistols and rifles. He looked over his shoulder towards the saloon and then shrugged his shoulders and nodded. The next minute, the two of them were walking towards the alleyway, the guard still looking nervously over his shoulder.

'Get back and keep quiet,' whispered Bob, flattening himself against the wall. Mick the Miner positioned himself close to the corner, and as soon as Susie and the guard turned into the alley, he raised one of his massive fists and bopped the guard on top of his head. The guard crumpled to the floor without a sound.

'Sweet! Thanks again, Susie; now, you get back home before you get into trouble,' said Bob.

'It was nothing,' Susie said as she went to leave. 'Now you come up and see me sometime, you hear?'

Showdown At The Pink Elephant Saloon

We led our horses into the street, and crept cautiously down to the saloon. I tied Freecloud to the hitching rail and held on to Fortune as

Bob tiptoed up to the saloon doors, peered inside, and then trotted back to us.

'Ham's in there,' he said. 'He's sat at a long table with Mad Mickey and three others. The table is stacked full of money and they're busy counting it.'

'Shall we storm the place together, boss?' asked Mick the Miner.

'No, I mean to have some fun,' said Wild Bob, smiling and mounting his horse. 'You stay out here as backup, until I call you. You, Kid, you're coming with me,' and he leaned down and pulled me up onto the saddle behind him.

'Ready, Kid?' he asked with a grin, and before I had time to answer he sent Fortune crashing through the swing doors and galloping across the polished wooden floor of the saloon. We skirted around the side of the long, fancy table and skidded to a stop in front of an astonished Horatio Ham. The horse reared onto its hind legs and let out an ear-splitting whinny.

Mad Mickey McKay went for his gun, sending a stack of coins crashing down, rolling and spinning across the floor. Faster than a rattlesnake's strike, Wild Bob's own gun appeared in his hand, cocked and pointing straight at the Marshal.

'Guns on the table, boys, and no funny business,' said Bob, and the four men sat at the table did as they were told. 'Looks like you've been caught with your fingers in the till, Ham,' said Wild Bob.

'How dare you,' interrupted Marshal McKay, spluttering and turning puce with anger. I can see why they call him Mad Mickey McKay now; he was absolutely fuming! 'I'll see you get ten years for this, you no-good, low-down farm boy.'

'A farm boy without a farm,' Wild Bob corrected him. 'But we all know why that is, don't we, Ham?'

Mad Marshal Mickey McKay was absolutely fuming!

Ham shrugged. 'All is fair in business and war,' he sneered. Then, looking closer at Bob, he said, 'Are you wearing lipstick?'

'No, I'm not,' said Bob, angrily wiping a sleeve across his mouth. 'Don't try and change the subject. I suppose you think it's fair to commandeer all the money from Trouble Bank?' he asked, through gritted teeth.

'I own the bank; by my reckoning I can do what I like with the money,' smiled the oily Ham. 'I'm going to use it to build a marvellous parade of new shops and casinos, saloons and theatres. It's for the town's own good.'

'Shops that you will own, but paid for by the people; you'll bleed the town dry,' said Wild Bob accusingly.

'Oh no, not completely dry. I have to leave them some money to spend in my shops. It's called business,' said Horatio Ham with a face as innocent as a baby's. 'I'm a businessman. What would you have me do?'

'Give the people back their money,' demanded Wild Bob.

'I can't do that, Ffrance.'

'Well I can,' said Bob. 'Kid, gather up all the money and dump it back in that trunk.'

Clearing The Table

I jumped down from Wild Bob's horse and landed with a thump on the floor. Then, under the unwavering stares of Ham, Marshal McKay and the two other men, I gathered stack after stack of banknotes and armfuls of cash and dropped them into the massive metal trunk that stood by the table.

'I don't know how you think you're going to shift that trunk, Ffrance,' said Ham with a smirk. 'It took four of us to lift it onto a wagon and then two strong horses to pull the wagon here. I hope you've got a carthorse handy.'

'Something like that,' smiled Wild Bob. 'Mick,' he called. 'Come in here a minute.' The saloon doors burst open and in walked Mick the Miner, his legs as thick as tree trunks and his chest as wide as an ox. 'Just lift that trunk up, would you, Mick?' asked Bob.

Horatio Ham snorted in derision, but Mick walked around the trunk, inspecting it from every side. He got down on his haunches and carefully tested its weight; satisfied, he heaved the trunk onto his back without a second's hesitation.

'What do you want me to do with it, boss?' his deep voice rumbled.

'Take it to Rafferty's store and tell him to make sure everyone in town gets what they are owed,' Wild Bob replied, and as if he were carrying nothing heavier than a blanket roll, Mick the Miner strolled out of the Pink Elephant Saloon.

'Kid, use your rope skills and tie them up good and tight,' said Wild Bob, throwing down a long length of rope he had looped over the pommel of his saddle. I fished the hunting knife out of my rucksack, cut the rope into four equal lengths and started to loop one around Ham, tying him tight to his chair.

'You won't get away with this, Wild Bob,' said Horatio Ham, spitting with anger. 'Anyway, I'll just take the money back again.'

'That would be a big mistake,' said Wild Bob,

suddenly looking very dangerous and levelling his gun at Ham's head. 'I won't be as lenient a second time. So, you've got to ask yourself, punk – is it worth the risk. Well, is it, Ham?'

Horatio Ham stared back at Bob, his face livid and running with sweat, but he didn't say a word. Then, from down the road, we heard the sound of gunfire. Some of Ham's men had returned and were starting to make a nuisance of themselves.

'Time to go, Kid,' said Bob. 'Go outside and mount up.'

Stopped In My Tracks

'You'll pay for this, boy, you just see if you don't,' yelled Ham, straining at the ropes that bound him.

I don't think so, I thought as I ran outside and jumped onto the back of Freecloud; we're out of here! Oh, but if only I had looked more closely at my saddle, I might not have been so confident.

Looking back inside the saloon I saw Wild Bob have a few parting words with Ham and then, just for the fun of it and in true Daredevil style, he launched his horse into a mighty leap. With an ear-shattering whinny and a wild look in his eye, the horse cleared the great oak table, his hooves missing the top of Ham's head by centimetres, and came clattering out through the swing doors.

'Let's go, Kid,' yelled Bob and galloped away down Main Street. I kicked Freecloud and she streaked away at top speed. Bob was some way ahead of me and the other Desperados were on their steeds and firing a few parting shots at Ham's regrouped forces.

All of a sudden, I came to a juddering halt and found myself hanging in mid-air still astride my saddle, as Freecloud galloped away from under me. I came crashing down in a cloud of dust, and as the dust cleared I saw that the street ahead of me was deserted. The Desperados hadn't realized I was no longer on

Me →

← I get left behind!

rope tied to saddle

Saddle

Freecloud carries on!

weakened girth strap snaps.

the back of Freecloud, and the whole gang were disappearing back towards Destiny.

Looking down at my saddle, I could see what had happened. Someone had anchored one end of my lasso to a hitching post and the other end to my saddle. Then, by cutting part way through the girth straps, they had guaranteed I wouldn't be going anywhere. But who could have done it?

'Well, if it isn't the Lariat Kid,' said a voice, and turning round, I met the smug smile of Silas Ham, Horatio's spoilt brat of a son. 'Not quite so cocky now, are you?'

Trouble County Jail

The slimy Silas Ham!

So that's how I have ended up here, waiting for the special surprise that Horatio Ham has promised me.

I was completely winded when Ham Junior yanked me off Freecloud's back, and it wasn't hard for him to wrap my own rope around me and lead me like a pet dog, back into the Pink Elephant Saloon. How embarrassing; the Lariat Kid caught with his own lariat!

Horatio Ham is a big bully

Inside, Silas Ham tied me to a table leg and went over to free his father and the others. 'Did I do good, Pa?' he asked.

'You did just fine, my boy,' said Horatio Ham as he shook himself free of the rope and limped towards me. I smiled when I saw that his foot was still giving him trouble. 'As for you, Master Lariat,' he continued, 'you didn't get very far did you, you pesky varmint. What's more, your beloved leader didn't hang around to save you either, did he? Some friend he is.'

I knew that wasn't fair and that Wild Bob wouldn't have known Freecloud was riderless as she thundered along in his wake. I was sure that as soon as he realized the truth he would organize a rescue party. In the meantime I had more pressing things to worry about.

Marshal McKay came marching over, his face still red with anger and his fingers twitching above the guns that hung at his sides.

'Want me to finish him now, boss?' he asked. 'It would be a real pleasure!'

'Oh no, not yet. He might just tempt

Ffrance back into town to try and rescue him, and then we'll be more than ready for him and his dumb Desperados. Anyway, I have a big surprise waiting for this pest, early tomorrow morning.'

Marshal McKay gasped. 'You don't mean . . .' he began.

'That's exactly what I do mean,' said Ham with a chuckle. 'We already have one hapless victim, and I'm sure a second won't be unwelcome. Now, get him out of my sight; take him over to the jail and put an extra guard on. No, put ten extra guards on!'

McKay frogmarched me straight to the jailhouse. Once inside, he unhooked a ring of large keys from the wall, pushed me into an empty cell and locked the door.

'Welcome to Trouble's premier bed and breakfast establishment,' he grinned. 'Except there's no bed, and you're gonna be the breakfast!'

'What are you on about?' I said nervously.

'You'll find out soon enough! Bye bye,' said McKay and closed the door that separated the cells from his office.

A Prisoner In Trouble

It's been a long, long night but I don't really want it to end, because as soon as dawn breaks, I know that Ham will give me the big surprise he's promised.

My first impressions of my temporary home were not good. The walls, although wooden, are thick, and the only window is heavily barred. I have a companion, however; the young Indian brave I mentioned earlier, and I thought that at least I'd have someone to talk to.

'Hi, I'm Charlie Small,' I said to the boy. 'What are you in for?' But my question was ignored. He didn't even look in my direction, or give any sign that I existed. He just sat cross-legged on the floor, staring up at the ceiling.

'We might as well be friends, seeing as we're both in the same boat,' I said. 'Do you know what's going to happen tomorrow morning – the great surprise?'

Again the boy didn't answer, continuing to stare into space. Perhaps he's in shock, or in some sort of trance, I thought. Or perhaps he's just really unfriendly, so I've given up trying to talk to him and now I'm looking for a way to break out.

I've been through my rucksack, hoping that something in my explorer's kit would give me an idea how to escape from this cell, but everything I've tried so far has been useless. I've tried gouging my way through the timber walls, first with my hunting knife and then with the crocodile's tooth, but the timbers are far too thick.

A pebble has just flown through the bars of the window and landed with a smack on my head. OUCH! Who would do such a stupid thing? Hold on, though, there's a piece of paper wrapped around the stone. It must be a message from Wild Bob. All my troubles are over! Wait a minute and I'll see what it says . . .

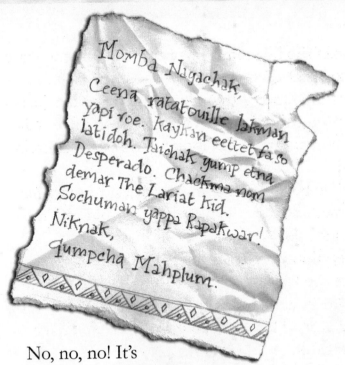

Momba Nyachak,
Ceena ratatouille lakman
yapi roe. Kayhan eettet faso
latidoh. Taichak yump etna
Desperado. Chackma nom
demar The Lariat Kid.
Sochuman yappa Rapakwar!
Niknak,
Qumpcha Mahplum.

No, no, no! It's
just a load of gobbledegook!
What am I going to do now? This *could* be
the last entry I ever make in my journal.

(If this is my last night, I'd just like to say
goodbye to my mum and dad, and thank you to
all the friends that have helped me on my
travels; Jakeman; Grip and Grapple; the Puffer
Fish Balloon; Jenny and her gran; the brave
Desperados. I would also like to say a big good
riddance to Thrak; the Perfumed Pirates; the
Puppet Master, and most of all Craik.)

Byeee!

Squashed Bug Alert!

Do not touch. This beetle can give you TERRIBLE diarrhoea. You have been warned!

Oops, sorry about that. Those two pages were stuck together with an ugly bug from Trouble Jail. But I'm not out of trouble yet. Far from it: I'm in more trouble than ever!

Hanging Around In Space

Whoa! Both the young Rapakwar brave and I are now suspended from the top of a high cliff in a rusty old cage, and we're waiting for Ham's surprise; and it's much worse than I ever imagined. My stomach flips over every time I think about it. It seems we are going to be . . . No sorry, I can't bear to even think about it.

There is nothing we can do but wait and hope that someone comes to rescue us. Though, if there is going to be any sort of rescue attempt, it had better be SOON!

Meanwhile, although my life is in the greatest peril, all I can do is bring my journal up to date, and describe how we got here. It's so annoying because less than an hour ago, we were so close to freedom…

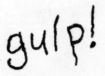

Nagachak

Who keeps shooting my journal?

My heart had sunk when I read the note wrapped around the pebble that came whizzing into our cell. It was just a load of nonsense. But maybe the note wasn't meant for me at all. I pushed it through the bars into the adjoining cell.

'I think this might be for you,' I said to the boy. He turned round and for the first time looked me in the eye. Then, without saying a word he took the piece of paper and started to read. He remained silent for a very long time. Finally, he spoke.

'You are one of Wild Bob's Desperados? You are Lariat Kid?'

'Yes,' I replied.

'Then I must apologize,' said the boy. 'My name is Nagachak, son of the mighty Rapakwar chief, Sitting Pretty. I thought you were a spy, put here to try and learn the secrets of the great Rapakwar nation.'

'Not me,' I said. 'I'm in for bank robbery, and first thing tomorrow, Ham has promised me a big surprise. I don't think it's going to be a nice one!'

'I have been promised this surprise also,' said the boy, looking worried. 'It is not good, I know.'

'What do you know?'

'We are . . .' Nagachak hesitated. 'Have you ever heard of Mapwai?'

'Mapwai!' I cried. There was that name again, the name that had scared Wild Bob so much. 'What is Mapwai?'

'Mapwai is a giant, bloodthirsty, gut-guzzling voracious vulture, also known as the Great Bird Of Death. To hear of her is scary enough. To see her, they say, is enough to drive strong men mad . . . and we are to be sacrificed to Mapwai, at dawn tomorrow.'

'*Sacrificed?*' I asked desperately. 'What do you mean sacrificed?'

'We are to be given to the giant bird for breakfast,' said Nagachak mournfully. 'Ham is full of superstitions, and believes that if he gives gifts to this disgusting bird, luck will always be on his side.'

'What does the note say,' I stammered, starting to panic. There is no way I wanted to end up as a huge bird of prey's bowl of Cheerios! 'Are they coming to rescue us?'

'This note is from my father. He is a great friend of Wild Bob Ffrance. They have spoken, and they are coming to rescue us . . . some time tomorrow.'

Help!

Big bird's breakfast

'What time tomorrow?' I cried. 'We're being sacrificed at dawn!'

'I'm afraid they don't say,' said Nagachak, screwing up the note and throwing it on the floor. 'Kid, if we want to escape we have to do it by ourselves.'

Escape From Trouble Jail

I couldn't believe it. Things were going from bad to worse.

'I don't know how we're going to get out of here,' I said. 'The walls must be made of solid tree trunks.'

'I know, but I have been studying this building,' said Nagachak. 'I think the weak point is the roof.'

I looked up into the gloomy roof-space, and noticed that although the rest of the building was solid and strong, the roof itself was made of a thick thatch – dried reeds that were laid over bare rafters.

'You're right. That's a bit of an oversight!' I said. 'So that's what you've been gazing at; I thought you were just staring into space.'

'If there is nothing other than the thatch, we might be able to squeeze through onto the roof,' said Nagachak.

'Brilliant,' I replied. 'But how do we get up there? It's mighty high.'

We tried running and jumping, but we were nowhere near reaching the roof. I put my hands through the bars and gave Nagachak a leg up, but he was still someway short of the beams. The bars themselves, although they went all the way up to the roof, were just too slippery to shin up. Then, looking through my rucksack once more, I thought I might have the answer.

I took out the ball of string and the glue pen. Turning the glue pen over, I read the blurb.

SUPER-STRONG, SUPER-FAST, SUPER-GRIP GLUE.

STICKS ANYTHING TO ANYTHING. YOU'LL BE AMAZED!

Right, I thought. Let's see if you're as good as you say! Starting about half a metre from the floor, I tied the loose end of the string to one of the bars with a special pirate knot, having first squirted the spot with a generous dab of glue. Then, unravelling the string, I knotted it tightly around the adjacent bar, which again I dabbed with the glue pen. Taking the string diagonally back to the first bar, I repeated the process, and continued zigzagging from one bar to the other as high up as I could reach. Like this:

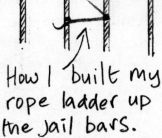

How I built my rope ladder up the jail bars.

Standing back, I looked at my handiwork. Excellent! I had made a rope ladder, and if the glue would hold, we should be able to climb up high enough to grab one of the rafters and squeeze through the thatch!

'Ready to give it a try?' I asked Nagachak.

'After you,' he said with a grin.

I put my foot on the lowest rung and gently applied my weight. The string was thin but strong, and although the knot slipped a bit, it soon gripped tight and I lifted myself off the floor. Carefully, I placed my other foot on the next bit of string. Again it held. It was going to work! Soon I had reached the top rung, my hands gripping the two bars in front of me.

Then, stretching up, I grabbed hold of one of the beams. I swung my feet back and then up, my legs bursting through the thatch of reeds. Letting go of the beam with one hand, I forced through the reeds and dragged the rest of me up and out onto

Beams

hole!

underside of thatch

me

I swing up and punch my legs through the roof

the rooftop. I immediately spread my weight over the thatch to stop falling back into the cell below, and parting some of the reeds, I looked down at Nagachak.

'It's easy,' I whispered. 'Come on!'

A few minutes later, Nagachak was beside me on the roof, and we were looking down onto a courtyard bathed in moonlight. In the courtyard were two guards, both with rifles. I put my finger to my lips and we set off silently along the roof towards freedom.

I Kick The Bucket

As quietly as mice we crawled along the rooftop and onto the next roof. The courtyard was on one side of us, where the two guards were talking in low voices; smoke drifted up from their disgusting cheroots. On the other side of the roof was a dark narrow alley, which we dropped down into as silently as shadows.

We ran to the end of the alley and looked out onto Main Street. The town was asleep, but outside the front of the jail stood a gang of guards. Nagachak and I looked at each other,

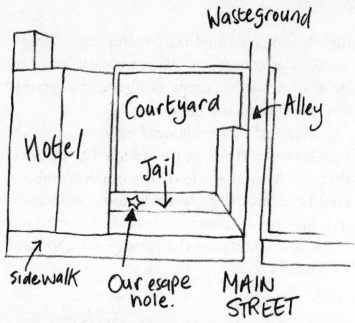

Wasteground

Courtyard

Motel

Jail

Alley

☆

Our escape hole.

sidewalk

MAIN STREET

shook our heads and scuttled back along the alley to the other end. This led onto a piece of wasteland on which stood a couple of run-down huts; beyond these was open country.

'Let's go,' said Nagachak and darted out into the moonlight and across the wasteland. His feet didn't make a sound in the dusty earth, and soon he was standing in the shadow of one of the huts. He gave a thin whistle for me to follow and I scurried out myself, feeling very exposed in the bright light of the moon. But nobody called; nobody challenged me, and I dived into the shadows alongside Nagachak, my nervous breath sounding loud in the still night air. We smiled at each other; we were going to do it! Carefully we crept along the side of the hut, invisible in the deep black shadow.

I still think it was a stupid place to leave a tin bucket! Right there, in the middle of the porch that ran down the side of the house. Anybody could trip over it in the dark, and somebody did. Me!

The bucket clattered and rang as it rolled across the wooden boards of the porch and immediately set the town dogs barking and howling. Nagachak and I were rooted to the spot, holding our

CLATTER
CRASH!

breath and praying that no one would bother to investigate the noise. It was a forlorn hope, because a light came on in the hut straightaway and we heard a voice call out.

'Who the dang-devil is out there, disturbin' of the peace? Where's my blunderbuss? You better watch out, you pesky prowlers. I'll blow you to kingdom come!' And the wall next to us was peppered with tiny holes as a mighty bang shook the hut.

'Run for your life!' yelled Nagachak as the door opened and a shaft of light fell across the porch steps. We ran.

'Hee, hee,' we heard the man cackle. 'I'm a comin' to get ya! This is better than a raccoon hunt.' The strange man wasn't the only one to come after us. We heard a yell go up amongst the guards at the jail, and we knew that they would be on our trail immediately.

Nagachak and I sprinted over the rock-strewn countryside. The moon had started to get low in the sky and soon it would begin to lighten with the dawn. 'We need a place to hide,' panted Nagachak. 'We'll be sitting ducks out here!'

I looked around frantically, not seeing any possible hiding place in the featureless, flat

WANTED
Charlie Small scrapbook!
Go to www.charliesmall.co.uk
and order your FREE copy –
then get cutting and sticking!

SCRAPBOOK
SOUVENIRS

Steering
wheel

PONY EXPRESS

Help!

BAKED
BEANS

Big bird's
breakfast.

Fantastic food for
explorers!

Lariat – A rope or lasso.

Lily liver – A coward.

Lingo – language.

Outlaw – A bandit.

Pard – Partner.

Ramuda – A herd of horses.

Red-Eye – Whiskey.

Saddle bum – A sort of cowboy tramp or drifter.

Six shooter – A pistol.

Stampede – A runaway herd.

Tack – A cowboy's working gear.

Vamos – 'Let's get out of here'

Wrangler – A cowboy

age

Chain

chak

ood
thin
the
of
ge.

bottom
swung
down.

Naga
fell to here and
climbed back up.

akeman's Patented Hydraulic Bison

Liquid pressure chamber incorporating pump

Hydraulic piston

Reservoir

Excess gas release valve

Thick leather hide, stitched and riveted

Main flywheel

Fast fuel fermentation tank

Heavy fur covering

Gas pressure pipes

Fuel intake

Leather Snout

Thick Hide

Brake

Foot rest

Control panel

Window slit

Cowhorn handlebars

Hatch

Passenger seat

Patent No. 102636

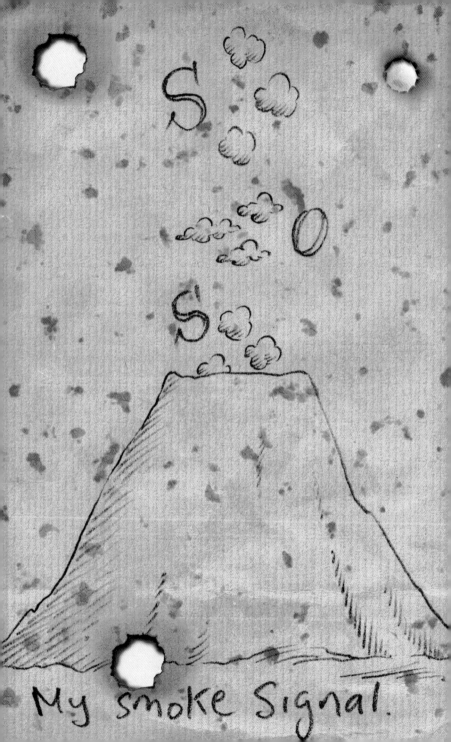

My smoke Signal.

landscape. The rocks were too small to hide behind and there were no trees to climb or caves to conceal us.

'It's no good,' I said. 'There's nowhere to hide. Oh, wait a tick!' I noticed a large, flat slab of rock sticking out where the ground rose in a deep step. Like this:

We crawled right to the back of the rocky overhang.

A Rattling Fun Time!

There was just enough room to crawl underneath the rock and hide in the deep shadows. We only just made it; as we scrambled back to where the rock met the earth, we heard the sound of men approaching. We were completely out of breath, and it took all our concentration to calm down and try to breathe quietly.

'They've got to be somewhere around here,'

said one voice. 'Bring the light over.' A man ran over with a flaming torch and they held it high and surveyed the landscape as they walked up and down. 'Nothin',' said the voice, and then louder he called, 'They're nowhere to be seen.'

'They can't have disappeared into thin air,' came a new voice and I recognized it at once.

'Horatio Ham,' I whispered. 'Now we're in trouble.'

'I want this whole area searched. We'll smoke 'em out if we have to. It'll soon be dawn and I need them for the great sacrifice.'

We waited in silence, a nervous sweat dripping down our faces as we heard the men start to search the area, kicking over stones and pulling up thin scrubby bushes. Then, as the sky started to turn silver in the approaching dawn, we heard Ham say, 'There, under that slab. Have you looked under there?'

'No, boss. It's too low for me to get under.'

'Then have a good feel around. They've got to be here somewhere.'

'But, boss, it's just the sort of place a rattler might hang out.'

'Do it!' said Ham, and I heard the sound of him drawing back the hammer on his pistol.

The next minute, a man's arm was nervously feeling about under the rock, and Nagachak and I held our breath as he felt the stones and twigs all around us. Then he grabbed my knee!

'I've got something, boss,' he cried as I quickly opened my rucksack and pulled out the bag of marbles I had bought in Granny Green's village.

'What is it?' demanded Ham.

'Not sure yet, boss, but it ain't no stone,' he said, squeezing my knee so hard I nearly cried out. Instead I lifted the bag of marbles and shook them hard. They rattled loudly.

'Oh no!' cried the man. 'It's a . . .' And at the same time Nagachak picked up a forked twig from the floor and jabbed it into the back of his hand. The hand was whipped away with a cry.

'I've been bitten! A rattlesnake has bitten me! I'm done for, boss.'

'Oh stop your whingeing and get yourself back into town.'

'I need to see the doc, boss. I need to see him quickly.'

'Do you think I'm made of money? I haven't got money to waste on doctors. What a lot of fuss over a little nip!'

We heard the man wander off, whimpering softly to himself, and as Ham and his men wandered away to continue their search elsewhere, Nagachak and I congratulated ourselves on our quick thinking.

A Rattling Bad Time

A rattling noise sounded again.

'It's OK, they've gone,' said Nagachak. 'You can put your marbles away now.'

'That wasn't my marbles,' I gasped and we both looked around in fear. We had celebrated too soon, for sliding through a small crack at the back of our hidey-hole, was a real rattlesnake! It was fat and angry, and it coiled up in front of us, its yellow eyes blazing and its tail rattling out an angry staccato.

Nagachak and I started to crawl slowly backwards out from under the rock, but the snake slithered round to cut off our escape. What now?

'How are we going to get out of this?' whispered Nagachak.

'I have no idea,' I replied. But even as I spoke I was gently searching through my rucksack again, trying not to make a sudden movement. My hand closed on the plastic lemon that I often used in my cooking, and just as I pulled it from the bag the rattler coiled back, ready to strike. I only just managed to unscrew the top when it struck at Nagachak. I squirted a stream of lemon juice straight at the snake's eyes

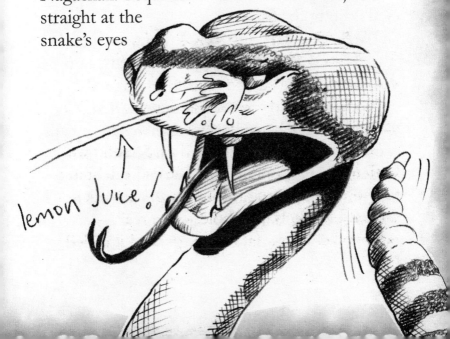

lemon juice!

and boy it must have stung, for the rattler coiled and writhed in pain. With an angry hiss, it quickly slithered away.

'Yahoo!' I cried.

'Shhh!' warned Nagachak, grasping my hand in thanks. 'Ham might still be around.'

'Sorry,' I whispered. 'Let's get out of here before the snake decides to come back.'

'Which one?' sniggered Nagachak as we backed out from under the rock, our eyes peeled for any further sign of the rattler. We both gave a huge sigh of relief as we emerged into the silver light of a beautiful dawn, but it froze in our chests as we turned around to see Horatio Ham and a line of his men, all armed and waiting for us.

'Well, look what just crawled out from under a rock,' said Ham with a sneer. 'And just in time for their special surprise. Grab 'em, men.'

Within seconds our hands were cuffed behind our backs and we were marched over to a covered wagon and hoisted on board. Half a dozen of Ham's men got into the back of the wagon to guard us, and the wagon started to move over the bumpy ground.

Caged!

Nagachak and I were driven fast across the countryside to the top of a high cliff looking out over a wide, sunken valley. Further along the cliff top we could just make out a tall rock, shaped like a crooked finger, pointing up into the sky.

'That's where Mapwai has his nest,' whispered Nagachak nervously.

Nearby, a big metal gantry hung out over the

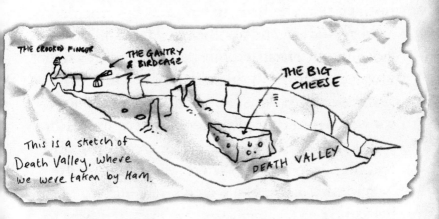

THE CROOKED FINGER

THE GANTRY & BIRDCAGE

THE BIG CHEESE

This is a sketch of Death Valley, where we were taken by Ham.

DEATH VALLEY

edge of the cliff and, from the end, a chain disappeared over the side. Mad McKay went over and started to turn a hand crank and, amidst much clanking and squealing of rusty wheels, a large and ornate metal cage rose into view.

'What do you think of my beautiful bird cage, Kid?' asked the unctuous Ham.

'Well, it's very rusty and there is no bird in it,' I replied, 'but apart from that, it's very pretty.'

'*You* go inside the birdcage, you dolt: you and this so-called son of a chief. Then the bird will come to you. And, for your information, that isn't rust all over the cage; it's dried blood. Ha ha ha ha!' Mean, vicious and downright bad, Ham started to laugh uncontrollably. 'Now get your sorry carcasses inside the cage,' he yelled, his face flushing with anger.

Mad McKay and another of Ham's hired gunslingers un-cuffed our hands and pushed us towards the cage at the edge of the cliff. Wow! My head started to spin when I saw how high we were from the valley floor. What's more, the valley appeared deserted; where were Wild Bob and the Desperados? Where was Sitting Pretty, Nagachak's dad? Why weren't they here to rescue us?

We were forced into the cage through a narrow doorway, which was locked securely behind us. Then McKay kicked the cage away from the cliff edge and we swung out over the void below. Again, with much squealing, the cage was lowered below the cliff ledge for about twenty metres.

The cage stopped and everything went silent. Nagachak and I sat on the barred floor of the cage, swaying high above the ground in the bright morning sunlight.

'What now?' I asked, but before Nagachak could answer, a cry came from the top of the cliff. It was Horatio Ham and he had started to chant:

Oh come great bird and accept this offering,
Oh come and feast on blood, guts and gore,
Two tender morsels I am offering,
With innards and entrails and claret galore.

A Quick History Lesson!

'What's he doing?' I asked.

'It's an old Rapakwar chant,' said Nagachak. 'In the old days my people thought the great bird represented both good luck and bad luck. I don't know why; perhaps because it has two heads.'

'Two heads!' I cried as a shudder of nerves went through my body. 'Nobody's mentioned two heads before.'

'Well, anyway,' continued Nagachak. 'They thought if they sacrificed a nice fat bison, Mapwai would bring them good luck instead of bad. It looks like Ham has gone one better and is offering human sacrifices.'

'But why should Ham care about the bird? He's not a Rapakwar.'

But to my great surprise, Nagachak replied, 'Well actually, he is. Sort of. Horatio Ham is my uncle.'

'Your uncle! And he's dangling you over a cliff as a treat for a monster two-headed bird? I don't understand. He doesn't look anything like a Rapakwar brave.'

'His father was not a Rapakwar. His name was Uriah Ham, a snake-oil merchant and scoundrel from back east, but he married the first daughter of Rolling Thunder, the old chief of the Rapakwar nation. One day, Uriah was caught stealing diamonds that came from the Rapakwar mines, and they were both banished along with

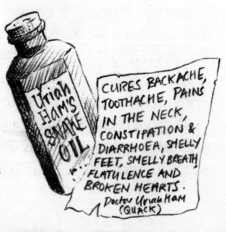

CURES BACKACHE, TOOTHACHE, PAINS IN THE NECK, CONSTIPATION & DIARRHOEA, SMELLY FEET, SMELLY BREATH, FLATULENCE AND BROKEN HEARTS.

Doctor Uriah Ham (QUACK)

Horatio, their newborn child.'

'You've got diamond mines?' I interrupted.

'Yes,' said Nagachak modestly. 'The Rapakwar have mined diamonds for centuries. We only use the stones for ceremonial purposes, and only we know the exact location of the mine entrance.'

'Wow! Oh, sorry, please carry on.'

'Well, Rolling Thunder had another daughter, my mum, and when she married Sitting Pretty, my father, he became chief of all the Rapakwar lands; Ham has been busy stealing them back ever since. But we still own the diamond mines and of course that is what Ham wants more than anything; the trouble is he doesn't know where they are. So he captured me and tried to make me give up our ancient Rapakwar secrets; but I didn't and that's why I am here now.'

'Rolling Thunder . . . diamond mines . . . banished?' I said. This was all too much and I was very confused. 'Why didn't you tell me all this before?'

'We were too busy escaping,' said Nagachak.

Even now that I've written it all down, it's hard to take in. Ham is Nagachak's uncle! Not only does he want to run Trouble County, he also wants the Rapakwar Indian diamond mines.

What's more, he's prepared to sacrifice his nephew, and me, to get them! Is there no end to his greed?

Now my journal is up to date and Nagachak and I are waiting for the arrival of the Great Bird of Death. I have no idea what to expect next. Will I end up as a piece of cuttlefish for an overgrown, two-headed budgie? How the heck are we going to escape from this?

Just now we heard an ear-splitting screech echo around the valley. 'Mapwai is coming,' Nagachak said.

Help! I don't know if I shall ever make another entry in my journal.

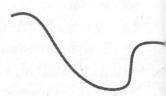

Help!

Ham the horrid!

Help!

Home sweet home!

Oh

Ouch!

If someone sent me a cake with a file in it, I could escape!

That hurts.

Come back Thrak,
all is forgiven!

AAARGH!

NO!

Is this what
the great bird of
death looks like?

Jeepers-Creepers

Marshal
McKay is
a nutter!

Wild Bob
where are yooooou!?

The Great Escape

PHEW, we made it. Just!

The screech echoed across the valley as Nagachak and I span helplessly in the metal birdcage, high above the valley floor. Again the screech came, and then a terrifying sound that reminded me of the sails of a pirate galleon thrashing to and fro in a full-blown gale. The next minute I saw Mapwai for the first time, and it is one of the scariest things I've ever seen. Nothing had prepared me for the horror that came spiralling out of the sky towards us.

The vulture was as big as a bus, its powerful body covered in tatty black and white feathers. Her legs were as thick as drainpipes and her feet tipped with twenty-centimetre-long talons. But the scariest things about the bird were the two viciously-beaked heads that were attached to the ends of her scabby pink necks.

(Now that I have time, I've looked through my animal collectors cards and, lo and behold, here is a card all about the Mapwai.)

THE MAPWAI

The Mapwai, or Great Bird Of Death, is a giant two-headed, vicious and bloodthirsty vulture from Rapakwar Indian mythology. Anyone who sees the Mapwai, usually ends up as her next meal. According to legend, the Mapwai was so greedy that she grew an extra head in order to eat even more. As a consequence, she has grown to an enormous size. Chance of escape: Nil.

WILD ANIMAL COLLECTORS CARDS

Bird Food !

The bird dropped from the sky as fast as a stone. Not braking or checking her flight in any

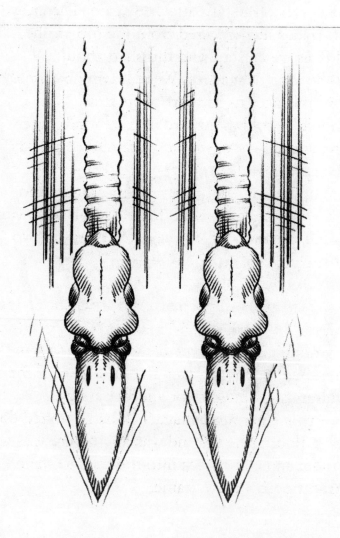

way, she slammed her feet into our cage, sending the whole crate rocking wildly on the end of its chain and we banged against the cliff wall. No sooner had we regained our shattered senses than the bird attacked again. The crowd of Ham's men cheered from the top of the cliff as we crashed and thrashed about.

'So long, Nagachak. We're leaving before the bird mistakes us for part of its treat. You should've told me where the diamond mines are, you silly boy,' shouted Ham, peering over the cliff edge. 'Oh, and good riddance to the Lariat Kid.' With this parting message, Ham pulled a lever and, with the sound of squeaking metal, the floor of our cage fell open on two rusty hinges.

YIKES!

My stomach flipped as I dropped out of the cage! At the last second I managed to grab the bottom bar, leaving me dangling by one arm, hundred of metres from the ground with the vulture swooping in for another attack.

I twisted around. Nagachak had grabbed the cage floor as he fell and was able to use it as a ladder and climb back into the cage to stand precariously on the frame.

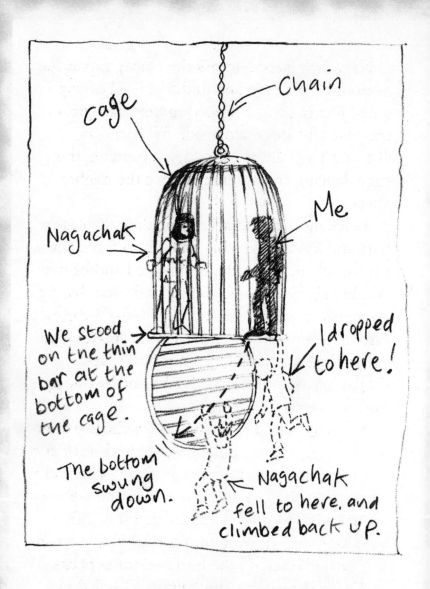

'Help, Nagachak,' I yelled, wriggling in mid-air like a worm on the end of a hook.

Nagachak leaped across the empty gap at the bottom of the cage and grabbed hold of my wrist. Just in time, I flipped myself back into the cage and stood alongside my friend as, *BANG!* The vulture hit us again, sending the cage dancing and spinning above the mighty abyss.

Twice more she attacked, bending the cage's bars and leaving gaps big enough to force her two deadly beaks through. Battered and bruised and breathing hard, Nagachak and I had hardly enough strength left to hold on. Now the great bird landed on an outcrop of rock about eight metres below us, stretched her necks, and darted her vicious orange beaks one by one up into the cage.

Nagachak and I both leaped for the top bars of the cage, quickly pulling our legs clear of the clattering beaks; but my jeans were ripped and my shin pouring blood from where the vulture scored a hit. Our arms started to burn with exhaustion as we hung on for dear life, our feet just out of reach of the bird's scything pecks.

'I'm going to drop any minute,' I yelled to Nagachak. 'I just can't hold on.'

A Stone's Throw

The vulture struck again, but as she forced her beak into the cage a large stone whizzed through the air and, – *Whack!* – it hit the bird hard on the side of one of her heads.

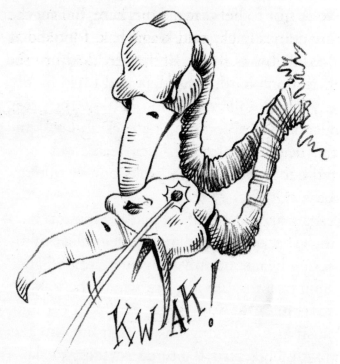

KWAK!

Kwaak! The bird screamed, withdrawing her beak and gazing down into the valley below. Another stone sailed through the air, hitting the

vulture on her other head. *Kwaak!* The huge
vulture scanned the valley with her cruel eyes
and, spotting something, spread her wings and
silently glided away from the rock.

Nagachak and I lowered ourselves until we
stood on the frame of the cage once again,
shaking with relief.

'We've got to get down from here, before the
vulture comes back,' said Nagachak. I looked at
the void below our feet, all the way down to the
valley floor.

'Any ideas?' I asked. Just
then, an arrow whipped
past my ear and
clattered through
the bars. 'Oh
brilliant, now
someone's shooting at us as well!'

A Leap Of Faith

'It's my father's arrow,' gasped Nagachak,
squatting down and picking up the missile. A
rope was tied to the shaft of the arrow and it
passed back through the bars all the way down

to the valley floor below. 'What are we supposed to do with it?'

'Look!' I cried, 'there's a note wrapped around the arrow.' With one hand holding the bars, I squatted down and tore the paper away.

But the message was written in Rapakwarian again.

'You'd better tell me,' I said.

Nagachak took the note and started to read.

'"Boys"' he read aloud. '"You must trust me. Tie the rope to your waists, cling together and JUMP!"'

'Jump!' I cried. 'Is he barmy? Can't we just tie the rope to the cage and climb down?'

'"You can't climb down,"' Nagachak continued reading. '"It is too slow and the Great Bird Of Death will pick you off like caterpillars on a cabbage stalk. Trust me, and jump. Love, Dad (Sitting Pretty, Chief.) PS Make sure the rope has passed over the frame of the cage before you leap!"'

'Let's do it!' cried Nagachak, and started to wind the end of the rope around his waist. It wasn't easy, balancing on the narrow bar of the cage and tying the rope at the same time. He wobbled and slipped and at one point I thought he was a goner, but at last he succeeded. As soon as he had finished, I took the excess that hung from his waist and wrapped it around me, tying it off with a double heave-ho knot, taught to me by the pirate Rawcliffe Annie.

'Ready?' he asked. I checked the rope at our feet, making double sure that it had passed through the bottom rung of the cage's frame.

'Ready,' I stammered, feeling anything but ready as we clung together.

'JUMP!' yelled Nagachak, and we jumped off the cage and out into thin air.

'*Aaaaaaaaaaaaaagh!*' We dropped like stones and I immediately wished I had not put my trust in Big Chief Sitting Pretty. I hadn't even met him and here I was jumping from a cage at the top of a cliff, just because he'd told me to. Next I'd be sticking my head in an oven for him!

Then, about halfway down, the rope tightened and our descent started to slow! How was that happening? And then I saw: Nagachak's dad had tied a boulder to the other end of the rope, one just a bit lighter than Nagachak and I together, and it acted as a perfect counter-weight to us. We glided down to the ground as sedately as if we were on an escalator. Brilliant!

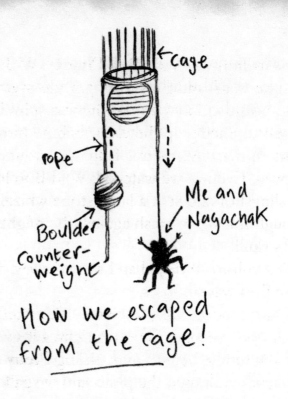

cage

rope

Boulder Counter-weight

Me and Nagachak

How we escaped from the cage!

The Great Chase

As soon as we touched down, Sitting Pretty ran over to us and cut us free with a slice of his knife. He was reassuringly calm, seemed very strong and looked both fierce and kind at the same time.

'Quick boys, follow me,' he said and led us through a maze of rocks until we were standing at the edge of the vast valley floor. Galloping towards us at breakneck speed on his beautiful black stallion was Wild Bob Ffrance. With one hand he was leading a snorting, wide-eyed pinto pony, and in the other he was spinning a slingshot. Racing up the valley behind him and no more than five metres from the ground, was Mapwai. Even as we watched, Wild Bob loosed the slingshot and sent a large stone whizzing through the air, to crash against the mighty bird's skull.

The vulture shrieked and turned away, dazed. Now Bob was upon us.

'Quick, mount up,' he yelled. 'We've only got a matter of seconds.' He was right. I leaped into the saddle behind him; Sitting Pretty and Nagachak mounted the pinto and we galloped off, just as Mapwai regained her senses and took up the chase once again.

Then I saw our horses were each dragging the bloody carcass of an old steer as extra bait for the vulture.

'Is that wise?' I shouted at Wild Bob as we thundered over the rocky ground. 'Isn't that just encouraging it?'

'Sure thing, Kid,' Bob yelled back. 'But don't worry. The Chief and I have a plan, and it's real sweet! Just sit back and enjoy. Yee-hah!'

We galloped away, around a curve in the cliff wall and out across the open valley floor. I could hear the great scything beats of the vulture's wings as she powered through the air behind us.

'Faster,' I yelled, urging Fortune on. 'Faster, or it's curtains for us all!'

The black stallion's hooves drummed on the hard mud, sending great billowing clouds of dust into the air. In front of me sat Wild Bob Ffrance, eyes wide with excitement. To our side raced Sitting Pretty and Nagachak. Behind each horse, the old cattle carcasses bounced and bucked in our wake.

'Not much further now, Kid,' yelled Wild Bob over the din of pounding hooves.

I do hope not, I thought, as I looked behind me. Mapwai was right on our tail. Her two heads rolled from side to side as she swooped over the rust-coloured earth and I heard the clack of her beaks as she lunged at the bloody bait we dragged behind us. All of a sudden Fortune reared as the vulture grabbed the carcass we were dragging, bringing us to a juddering halt.

'Come on!' cried Wild Bob, kicking the stallion back into a full gallop and snatching the meat out of the vulture's beak. 'Don't give up now!'

We raced away, and there directly in front of us was the great wedge of rock known as the Big Cheese. The rock rose sheer and high from the valley floor and tapered to a viciously sharp edge – and we were racing straight towards it. Again I heard the hollow clack of the vulture's beaks right behind us and, as the bird let out an ear-splitting screech, I nearly fell from the horse in fright.

I really didn't think we were going to make it!

Divide And Rule

We galloped towards the knife-edge corner of the Big Cheese. One head of the vulture snapped at the carcass Bob and I were dragging; its other head snapped at the carcass dragged by Sitting Pretty's pinto. Still we galloped on, straight towards the huge rock.

'Turn, Bob. Turn!' I yelled. Surely we were going to be dashed against the lethal rocks that littered the ground around the base of the Big Cheese! 'Help!' But Bob didn't turn and we raced on towards a certain and sticky end!

Then at the very last second, when the black stallion was already stumbling over a fall of loose stones and the Big Cheese loomed massive in front of us, Wild Bob yanked on the reins and our faithful steed turned and galloped madly along the side of the colossal outcrop. As we turned to the right, Chief Sitting Pretty turned to the left and hurtled along the other side of the rock. The monster vulture tried to follow both of us! Her right head, snapping at the steer that Bob was dragging, followed us to the right; the bird's left head followed Sitting

Pretty's steer to the left, and at full speed the vile vulture hit the knife-sharp edge of the Big Cheese!

With an awful *Kreeeeeeech*, the bird was rent asunder, splitting right down the middle, and her two halves dropped heavily to the ground on either side of the rock. There was a sudden silence except for our gasping breath. It was over! We were saved! Bob pulled his sweating, snorting stallion to a halt.

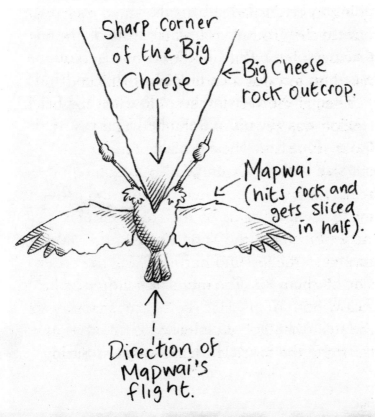

Sharp corner of the Big Cheese

← Big Cheese rock outcrop.

← Mapwai (hits rock and gets sliced in half).

↑ Direction of Mapwai's flight.

'Ooee, that must have stung,' said Bob grinning, but strangely I couldn't help feeling sorry for the creature. Yes, she had tried to kill me; she had tried to strip the flesh from my bones, but that's only what vultures do, isn't it? It wasn't her fault. Then as we trotted alongside the remains of the monster and I saw her massive curved beak and her pitiless, wicked eye, I breathed a huge sigh of relief. No, I wasn't sorry at all; hot-diggity-dog – she had tried to peel me like a banana!

Sitting Pretty and Nagachak trotted around the edge of the Big Cheese to join us. Nothing was said; we were all a little shell-shocked and were only just realizing how close we had been to a very nasty end. We climbed a narrow path out of Death Valley and made our way back to Destiny.

Celebration

The Desperados all cheered as we rode back into Destiny.

'How did it go, boss?' asked Gentleman Jim.

'It was real sweet, Jim, real sweet,' replied

Wild Bob. 'Horatio Ham has been foiled again and what's more, Mapwai, the Great Bird Of Death, has been slain!'

The Desperados cheered even louder, whooping and hollering and firing off their pistols.

'This calls for a feast,' declared Cornelius Duff, who already had an extra large pot of baked beans bubbling on the campfire. Soon, with the help of a large bottle of firewater, the Desperados and Chief Sitting Pretty were dancing a Rapakwar victory dance around the roaring campfire, waving rifles and tomahawks, and chanting *The Mapwai is dead, the Mapwai is dead, Ee-I-Adio the Mapwai is dead!*' Then, when they were too tired to dance anymore, Cornelius Duff dished out the beans and, as a special treat, a big bowl of cactus soup (yum yum, I don't think!).

We had speeches and songs and Chief Sitting Pretty told the whole saga of our fight with Mapwai (which was a bit boring as he spoke in Rapakwar, and I didn't understand a word!). Then the pipe of peace was passed around, to strengthen the friendship between the Desperados and the Rapakwar nation.

'No thanks,' I said when the pipe was passed to me. 'I don't smoke.'

'You must,' whispered Wild Bob. 'Otherwise the Rapakwar will take it as a great insult. Just take a little puff.'

Really disgusting Pipe of peace!

I put the pipe to my lips and as the disgusting green smoke floated around my head, I sucked. The evil-smelling smoke hit the back of my throat. It was disgusting – hot, rough and sour – and I instantly collapsed in a fit of uncontrollable coughing. The Desperados roared with laughter but as my head cleared and I could see their friendly faces through my watery eyes, I laughed too; it felt so good to be a Daredevil Desperado!

All too soon though, it was time for Nagachak and his dad to go. Chief Sitting Pretty, the proud and implacable warrior chief who looked as if he had been carved out of solid rock, put his hand on my shoulder.

chief Sitting Pretty

'Nagachak has told me how you helped him to escape, Kid Lariat. You have proved yourself a worthy friend and I now make you an honorary Rapakwar Brave.' With this, he took one of his many bead necklaces and placed it around my neck. 'Good luck, brother. If you ever need my help, send a message and I will come.'

'Wow! Thank you,' I said, beaming with pleasure at this unexpected honour.

'Goodbye, Kid,' said Nagachak with a smile, and shook my hand. They mounted their horse; Chief Sitting Pretty flicked the reins, and amidst much cheering, the pinto raced out of Destiny.

As I watched them go, I wondered how long it would be before *I* would be able to leave and continue my journey home. We had escaped the Great Bird Of Death, but horrible Ham was still about, lording it over the poor people of Trouble County. Before I could go I had promised to help defeat him. To be honest, I was beginning to wonder if that would ever happen.

As I made my way back towards the bunkhouse, I glanced down at the necklace the

Chief had just given me, and gasped. It was made up of hundreds of brightly-coloured beads, but there in the middle, sparkling in the morning sun, was a diamond as big as a walnut!

Wow! Chief Sitting Pretty gave me a diamond as big as a walnut!

Sleep Glorious Sleep!

Now my journal is right up to date, and it's time for bed. I'm absolutely exhausted, and I ache all over. No one wake me up for a week!

zzzᶻzzzᶻᶻz!

Later

You'll never guess where I am now. No, really, you'll never, ever guess. I can hardly believe it myself. I'm deep down inside the bowels of the earth, looking through a crack in a rock at a scene illuminated by the glow of a thousand oil lamps!

First, though, I must tell you all about the big showdown between the Daredevil Desperados and Horatio Ham's Hired Honchos! All about my meeting with . . . No, let me continue from where I left off.

Invitation To A Fight

'Kid! Kid Lariat, wake up.'

'Wha . . . ?'

'Wake up, Kid. It's time to go.' It was Wild Bob Ffrance.

'Time to go where? I've only just this minute dropped off to sleep,' I complained.

'You've been asleep for two days, Kid,' chuckled Bob. 'Now get up. We've got an appointment to keep.'

'What appointment?' I asked, still very fuzzy

in the head. I hadn't made any appointments.

'Shake a leg and I'll tell you all about it while you're getting dressed,' said Wild Bob.

I stumbled out of my bunk and pulled on my jeans. The hut was deserted and I could see through the windows that the sun was already high in the sky. 'What's going on?' I asked.

'When we got back from Death Valley, I held a meeting with the rest of the Desperados,' said Wild Bob. 'They were horrified when they learned what Ham had tried to do to you and Nagachak and we decided that enough is enough! Our little raids have had no effect whatsoever. We must try and destroy Ham's power base once and for all. To that end, I sent Ham an invitation, an invitation I'm glad to say he has accepted.' With these words, Wild Bob handed me this scrap of paper:

TO HORATIO HAM,
THIS FEUD HAS RUMBLED ON LONG ENOUGH.
LET'S GET IT SORTED.

You are cordially invited to a once-and-for-all showdown between you and the Desperados.
Time: 17th of the month at 12 Noon.
Place: The Wasteland. Prize: Winner takes all.
RSVP.
BRING YOUR OWN GUNS.

Let's get ready to rumble!

'Wow!' I cried. 'A final showdown. That's a bit drastic. What happens if you lose?'

'Losing is not an option,' said Wild Bob, somewhat grim-faced. 'But we've got to face the fact that we might well lose. Sneaky Pete has been out sneakin' around, and has just reported back that Ham has a gang of hired gunslingers over five hundred strong.'

I whistled. 'That's one heck of a lot of men. How many do you have on your side?'

'Well, all in all, counting you, about twenty,' said Bob.

'Twenty!' I cried. 'We'll be driven out of this state and into the middle of next week!'

'We might be driven out of this life altogether,' said Bob. 'So I just want to say, you've been a real pal and I've no right to ask you to fight my battles for me. If you want to get going on your journey, no one will hold it against you.'

But I didn't even need to think about it. 'You saved my life, and there's no way I'm going to let you and the rest of my pals face Horatio Ham without me,' I said, and immediately thought, whoops, that was a bit hasty!

'Good lad, I knew we could count on you,'

said Wild Bob, smiling broadly. 'Now, you'd better get ready.'

'How many days until the seventeenth?' I asked, wondering how long I had got to hone my lariat skills.

'Erm,' said Bob. 'Today is the seventeenth!'

'Today!' I cried. Hot-diggity-dog! 'And what's the time now?'

'It's eleven o'clock,' said Bob, standing up to leave. 'We've got one hour until showtime! I'll let you finish getting ready. I've got some last minute things to deal with.'

I said who keeps →ㅤshooting my Journal?!

Sending Signals

One hour? ONE HOUR! What on earth was I going to do? I hadn't come all this way to be blasted into eternity by a power-crazed son of a snake-oil merchant; but I had also given Wild Bob my word that I would stay and fight. We needed help. We needed reinforcements, but how on earth was I going to get any? Then I remembered Chief Sitting Pretty's promise. He would help; he said he would. All I had to do was send him a message . . .

I staggered bleary-eyed into the sunshine, and the first thing I saw was the campfire in the middle of the compound sending a plume of smoke into the sky. That's it, I thought. A smoke signal – I'll send a smoke signal. Hold on, though. I don't know how to do it! Never mind, I thought, I'll have to use Morse code instead and just hope the Rapakwar warriors understand and come running! I ran back into the bunkhouse for my blanket and dampened it under the camp pump. Now, I thought, let's see if this works.

'Could you give me a hand, Mr Duff?' I asked.

'Of course, my dear,' said the kindly corpulent cook, putting down his tea-towel and waddling over.

'If you just stand on one side of the fire and hold the corners of this blanket, I'll do the rest,' I said. Holding the blanket low over the smouldering cinders, we lifted it once, twice, three times. Each time, a separate puff of smoke drifted up into the air, higher and higher until it passed through the mouth of the volcano. We did three small puffs, three large puffs and then another three small ones.

My smoke signal.

Dot-dot-dot. Dash-dash-dash. Dot-dot-dot. SOS!

Oh, I hope the Rapakwar receive the signal . . . and understand it!

'Are you ready, Kid?' shouted Wild Bob from over by the corral. 'It's time to go.'

An Appointment With Fear

The Daredevil Desperados were all waiting for me, so I slung my rucksack on my back and mounted Freecloud, who had followed Wild Bob all the way home after dumping me in the Main Street of Trouble town.

I grabbed one of the bacon sarnies that Cornelius Duff was handing out, and wolfed it down. I was starving, but either the bacon had gone off or I was getting really scared, because my tummy started to burble like a pan of his bubbling baked beans!

Solemnly we rode two abreast up the steep path, through the tunnel and down the hidden track to the outside of Destiny volcano. The Desperados were armed to the teeth with rifles and pistols and slingshots and blunderbusses, but they knew it would never be enough against Ham's hordes. The Daredevils were going to fight a losing battle, but they had a job to do and would do it to the best of their ability. My knees were knocking against Freecloud's side as we kicked our horses into a gallop and rode off towards the wasteland.

Ham's Hordes

The blood froze in my veins when we arrived at the wasteland, a huge and rocky open area. Silhouetted against the skyline, on the other side were Horatio Ham's henchmen, all five hundred of them. Our little band of Desperados looked pathetic in comparison. How on earth were we going to escape from this deadly confrontation? Where were the Rapakwar Indians; had Chief Sitting Pretty understood my message?

I looked at Wild Bob Ffrance. Had he any ideas? When I saw his face, I could see that he hadn't. He caught my questioning look.

'Don't worry, Kid, something always turns up when you least expect it.'

'Like the Rapakwar Indians?' I asked.

'How do you mean?'

'I sent them a message, but they don't seem to have received it.'

'Never mind, I don't think they would be the answer,' Bob said, smiling.

'Why, I thought a tribe of warrior braves would be just the thing!' I said, feeling a bit put-out. Then, as a bloodthirsty call sounded from the low ridge to our left, I saw what Wild Bob meant. There, on the backs of their war-painted ponies, longbows over their shoulders and tomahawks in hand, were the Rapakwar braves. All twelve of them, and apart from Sitting Pretty and Nagachak, the rest were as skinny and stooped as their longbows and as toothless as toads. They were wrinkly old granddads!

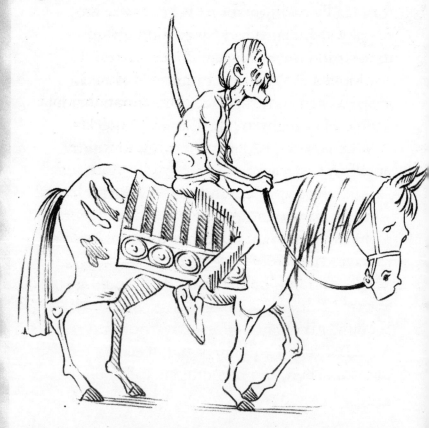

'Is that it; is that all they sent?' I gasped.

'That, I'm afraid, Kid, is the entire male population of the Rapakwar nation. And that's why I didn't bother asking for their help!'

Brilliant, now we're really done for!

Parley

I thought to myself: I've got to try and stop this madness before the obnoxious Ham defeats the brave Daredevil Desperados. I would put a stop to it, right now: I would demand a pow-wow! Surely this situation could be resolved by talking it through? I quickly opened my rucksack and felt around inside until I found my white scarf (well, white and blue, really). Then carefully and quietly, I leaned over and withdrew the rifle from the holster on Gentleman Jim's saddle. I tied the scarf of truce to the end, and holding it high in the air, I gave Freecloud a kick and sent her galloping into the middle of the wasteland.

My flag of truce.

'Come back, Kid,' yelled Wild Bob. 'It's no good, they won't listen.'

'I've got to try,' I shouted over my shoulder as I brought Freecloud to a halt in the middle of the arena, facing Ham's army of thugs. My heart was pounding against my ribcage, and my hands were clammy with fear. Now it was up to Ham to send a negotiator out to talk to me. Already, I could see Ham talking to a group of his men. Perhaps this was going to work. Then, quite unexpectedly, I heard a low rumble of thunder. That's strange, I thought, looking at the sky, there isn't a cloud to be seen.

The rumble grew louder and louder as one of Ham's men galloped out to meet me. This is more like it, I thought. Now we're getting somewhere. Imagine my surprise then, as the rider swung his rifle out of its holster, and at full gallop, aimed and fired, blasting a huge hole in my scarf of truce! Yikes, Bob was right. These men weren't prepared to talk. It's time to get out of here. Now!

I turned Freecloud around, ready to scarper, but as I did so the rumble of thunder became deafening and the ground beneath our feet started to shake violently. Over to my right, a huge dust cloud hung in the air. What was it; an earthquake; a vast army of tanks? I started to shake as violently as the ground – this was terrifying!

The rifleman seemed just as frightened, made a U-turn and retreated into the distance. The dust cloud grew closer and closer and the ground started to shake even more. It was getting hard to stay on Freecloud. What the heck was going on – had Destiny erupted?

Ham's man had had the right idea; it was time to go. I gave Freecloud a kick, but now the ground was shaking so much I couldn't hold on, and as Freecloud galloped off towards the Desperados, I was shaken out of the saddle and landed with a thump on the ground. Again!

I got to my feet quickly. The cloud of dust was now only a couple of hundred metres away and closing fast. Then, as a breeze parted the billowing clouds for a second, I could see what was hurtling towards me. Bison, a hundred thousand strong! I was rooted to the spot in the path of a gigantic bison stampede. HELP!

The dust cloud parted...

Swallowed Up In A Bison Stampede

There was nothing I could do. Even if I ran I couldn't reach the end of the humungous herd before it was upon me. I was going to be trampled as flat as a piece of paper.

'Kid!' I heard Wild Bob cry above the cacophony of half a million thumping hooves, but then I was swallowed up in the great, swirling fog. The dust filled my nose, the noise filled my ears and the last thing I saw before I closed my eyes, was the massive leader of the herd dip its head, ready to strike. His woolly head was as broad as an armchair, his horns as thick as Thrak's mighty arms. I squeezed my eyes shut and braced myself for the collision. Aaargh, here goes!

But the strangest thing happened. I felt the lightest of bumps from the great bull's head as it gently scooped me from the floor with its horns. With a toss of its head I was sent spinning through the air. I braced myself for the crushing thump as I bounced off the bison's back and fell under the herd's pounding hooves . . . but the next minute I found myself sitting on a stool next to a very strange little man indeed!

What on earth was going on?

Jakeman's Patented Hydraulic Bison

I looked round in disbelief. The man next to me was very short, hardly any taller than me, and had an enormous peppery brown moustache sprouting from under his bulbous nose. On his head he sported an old flying cap and a pair of oily goggles.

This was totally bizarre: who was he, and how did I get here? One minute I had been stuck in the path of a bison stampede in the middle of the dusty wasteland, and the next it was as if I had been suddenly plucked from the earth by a passing spaceship. Maybe I had! I started to panic.

I was sat next to a very strange little man.

'What's going on?' I cried above the noise of thumping pistons and hissing airbrakes. 'Where am I?'

'Just a minute, Charlie!' said the strange man, frantically pressing buttons and pulling levers.

Hold on! How did he know my name? This was getting weirder by the minute!

'Ah, that's better. So glad you could drop in, Charlie! I've been looking all over the place for you.'

'You have?' I asked in amazement. 'But who are you and how do you know my name; are you some sort of alien who's beamed me up into their flying saucer?'

'No, I'm not an alien and you're not in a spaceship,' chuckled the little man, adjusting his goggles. 'You're . . . yikes! That was a close one.' He twisted the throttle grip on a pair of cow-horn handlebars and with a smart double-declutch, he changed gear and our mysterious craft accelerated away to the sound of screaming machinery.

The man reached under his seat and pulled out a sheet of paper. 'This might explain where you are,' he said.

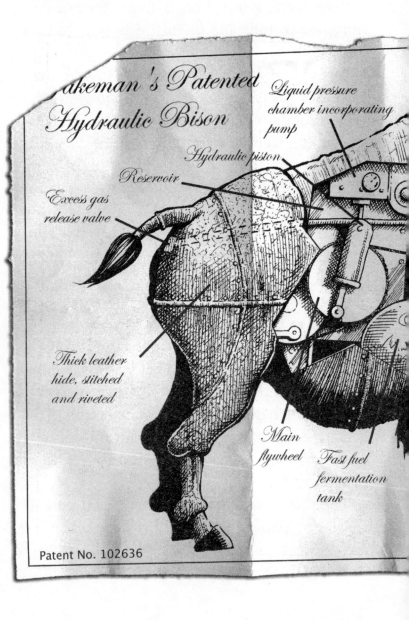

...akeman's Patented Hydraulic Bison

Liquid pressure chamber incorporating pump

Hydraulic piston

Reservoir

Excess gas release valve

Thick leather hide, stitched and riveted

Main flywheel

Fast fuel fermentation tank

Patent No. 102636

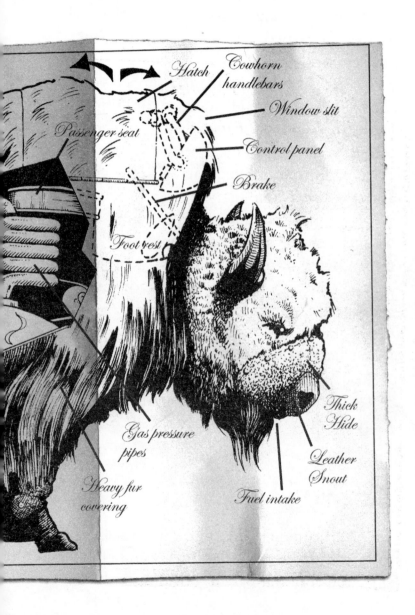

Cowhorn
handlebars

Hatch

Window slit

Passenger seat

Control panel

Brake

Foot rest

Thick
Hide

Gas pressure
pipes

Leather
Snout

Heavy fur
covering

Fuel intake

'It's another one of Jakeman's mechanical animals,' I gasped. 'Oh! Do you mean I'm inside this bison?'

'Correct,' smiled the man. 'I flipped you over the bison's head, you landed on the spring-loaded hatchway in its back and dropped down into the seat next to me. Pretty nifty bit of driving, don't you think; you do know who I am now, don't you?'

'No,' I said, looking at him carefully. 'Have we met before?' I'm sure I would have remembered a strange little man like this.

'Oh, come on, Charlie. You're not usually so slow!' said the man, pointing at the diagram of the hydraulic bison again. 'Have a guess.' And then I had it. Of *course*, it was obvious!

'You're Jakeman!' I cried.

'Correct,' chuckled the man. 'And it's so nice to meet you at last, Charlie Small.'

Jakeman!

Yippee! I couldn't believe it. I was finally face-to-face with the man who had been helping me since the very start of my adventures. I had

ridden his steam-powered rhinoceros across the
endless plains towards the gorillas' jungle;
driven his jet-propelled swordfish through
stormy seas; sunk an enemy ship with his
clockwork limpets and been saved from certain
death by the monstrous hydro-electric
submawhale. And here was the man who had
invented all those wonderful machines.

'This is brilliant! I've been desperate to meet
you,' I cried, and all the questions that I had
been bottling up inside for so long, came
pouring out. 'How come you keep helping me,
Mr Jakeman; do you know how I ended up in
this strange world; can you tell me how to get
home?'

'Slow down, slow down, Charlie my boy. Yes,
I can answer all of your questions . . . but later.
First we've got a job to finish.'

'We have?' I asked. In all the excitement of
meeting Jakeman, my mind had become a
jumble, and I had no idea what I was supposed
to be doing.

'Of course, you haven't forgotten Horatio
Ham have you? Look!' Jakeman pointed out of
the small slit of a window in front of us and I
could see we were charging straight towards

Ham and his horde of hired guns. 'I'm the lead bison in this stampede,' he added. 'And wherever I go, the herd will follow.'

He throttled the bison up and we powered forward even faster, and from the noise coming from behind us, I knew that the rest of the huge herd was following.

Operation Demolition

'Just a minute, the view's a bit restricted in here,' said Jakeman and with a flick of a switch the hatch doors swung open, our seat was raised, and we could peer out over the top of the hydraulic bison's powerful shoulders. Brilliant!

Ham's men were panic-stricken. Some were mounting their horses to escape, some just running away on foot, and in the middle of them all, Horatio Ham stood stock-still with a look of complete disbelief on his face.

'Run, Ham, run!' I yelled, standing up so that the top half of my body was sticking out of the bison. Goodness knows what Ham was thinking. Perhaps his mind was a complete blank. I'm not exactly sure what happened next, but as we galloped straight at Ham, I heard a whoop and a yell from behind us. I turned to see Wild Bob Ffrance, the Daredevil Desperados and the Rapakwar warriors joining the back of our stampede.

'Come on, Bob. They're on the run!' I yelled, but when I turned forwards again, we had passed right over the spot where Ham had been standing and I could see neither hide nor hair of him. Whoops! Had we pummelled him as flat as a very flat pancake?

I had no time to think, for Jakeman turned the bison stampede straight towards Ham's ranch, Two-Eyes. It must have changed a great deal since Wild Bob's parents had owned it, because now a huge and gaudy mansion stood on the land. But not for long!

'Heads down, closing hatchway,' called

Jakeman and I sat back down as the seat lowered and the hatch closed. 'Hold on tight, this is going to be a rocky ride,' he chuckled.

We hit the wooden homestead at full pelt, the rest of the bellowing buffaloes right on our heels. To the thunderous sound of splintering wood and crashing furniture, we ploughed right through the mansion. Ham's headquarters were history.

Mission accomplished!

So Long To The Desperados

It takes a long time to stop a bison stampede,
and when Jakeman finally brought the huge
herd to a standstill, we were a good half
kilometre beyond Two-Eyes. As the snorting,
panting bison herd lowered their heads to feed
on Ham's lush pasture, Wild Bob and his men
rode up.

'Yippee! I've never seen anything like it!'
cried Wild Bob. 'Who's your pal, Charlie?'

'This is Jakeman,' I exclaimed. I was so
thrilled at having met Jakeman, and by our
battle with Horrible Ham, that my words came
pouring out so fast they started tripping over
one another in the rush. 'He's the man I told
you about; theonewhobuiltallthosemarvellous
mechanicalbeasts, he's . . .'

'Slow down, Kid,' said Bob with a smile.
'Where did you spring from, partner?' he asked
Jakeman.

'Oh, a long way away,' said Jakeman quietly.
'Miles away; worlds away!'

'Well, I'm mighty pleased to meet you, sir,'
said Bob. 'You were brilliant, both of you,' and

as the Desperados cheered and threw their hats into the air in celebration, Chief Sitting Pretty, Nagachak and the small band of wrinkled warriors immediately went into their victory dance, whooping and chanting.

'Have we done it, then?' I asked Bob above the noise. 'Has he gone?'

'I should say so. I saw him run like a jackrabbit, just before you hit. He ran to the ridge and left in a wagon with his slimy son, Silas. Don't worry; we won't be seeing him again. He looked scared half to death! Yee-hah, we've won!' crowed Wild Bob and joined in the Rapakwar dance, stamping his feet and shouting at the sky.

'What now?' I asked when the celebrations had subsided. 'Are you going back to Destiny?'

'No need to, Kid. We've won. We can all go home. Well, I'll have to rebuild mine first, of course,' he said looking down the slope to the pile of shattered wood where the ranch used to be.

'That's no problem, though. I wouldn't

(Not so cocky now, are you Silas?)

want to live in Ham's ghastly palace; and I'd be mighty proud, Kid, if you'd stay and help.'

'Oh, that won't be possible, I'm afraid,' said Jakeman. 'I'm going to show Charlie . . . I mean the Kid, how to get back to his own home.'

'Oh, wow! Do you mean it, Mr Jakeman; you're going to show me the way home?'

'Of course, Charlie my boy. Why do you think I've come all this way – just to say "How do you do?"'

'Oh, brilliant!' I cried, leaping up and down in excitement. 'I'm going home!'

'Well, I'll miss you, Kid. You've been a real pal and no mistake. We couldn't have done it without you,' said Wild Bob, mounting Fortune and leaning forward to shake my hand. 'Now you take care, you hear? I hope you make it home. So long, partner.'

With a wave Wild Bob led the others back towards Two-Eyes.

Goodbye, Bob.

On My Way Home

Jakeman and I climbed back into the hydraulic bison, and as he set the machine in motion, I turned in my seat and waved as the Daredevil Desperados, and the Rapakwar Braves disappeared down the hill. I will miss them very much, they were all such good friends; but the best amongst them, and the one I'll miss the most is Wild Bob Ffrance.

Jakeman steered the bison at a trot across the open ground at the top of the hill, and soon we passed through a ravine and out across an arid stretch of ground that quickly turned into a desert. I was feeling sad about leaving my good friends behind, but I was also really, really excited about meeting the marvellous Jakeman. There was so much I needed to ask him.

'It's brilliant of you to help me like this,' I said, as soon as we were on our way.

'Think nothing of it, Charlie my boy,' he said with a smile.

'And you're sure you can help me get back to my mum and dad?'

'Yes indeed,' he said. 'It's the least I can do.'

'What do you mean?'

'Ah, well,' said the little man, coughing and turning a little red. 'You could say, I suppose, that it was, um . . . a little bit my fault you ended up here at all.'

'Your fault that I sailed down a crocodile-infested river and had to arm-wrestle a huge silverback gorilla? How on earth could that be your fault?'

'Well, let me explain. It all started when I was trying to re-set the huge clock that sits on top of my factory. I had just . . .'

Whirr, chung, clunk!

'Oh no, what's that?'

There was a terrible grinding noise from the bison and we came to an abrupt and squealing halt. Jakeman jumped down and started to unscrew various plates underneath the heavy coat of the magnificent machine.

'I thought so,' said Jakeman, sighing. 'He's got sand in his joints. There's nothing I can do about it now; I'll have to send Philly, my assistant, to come and repair it later.'

'Oh, that's great!' I cried in frustration. 'Now I'll never get back home.'

'Calm down, Charlie,' said Mr Jakeman. 'Of

course you will. We're just going to have to walk a bit, that's all.'

'Walk!' I gasped in astonishment. 'Exactly how far is it?'

'To your home, you mean? Oh, you can't measure that in kilometres, Charlie. I'll have to do some inventing to get you back there, which means we must go to my factory first . . . and that's only about three thousand kilometres or so.'

'Only three thousand kilometres!'

'That's right. Come on, Charlie; the sooner we get started, the sooner we'll arrive. And I can explain all about how you got here, on the way. Best foot forward!'

Speechless, I jumped down to join him.

A Not So Helpful Hand

We set out across the desert sands under a blistering sun. It was hot and thirsty work; almost too hot and tiring to talk, but there were lots of things I needed to know.

'Who are you, Mr Jakeman; are you some sort of magician?' I asked, panting for breath.

'Goodness me no, Charlie, nothing like that!' he puffed. 'I'm a scientist and an engineer. Although some people might think that amounts to the same thing!'

We carried on trudging through the deep sand. It was so hot it felt like my brain was starting to fry. I wish I had put some sun block in my explorer's kit.

'So how could it be your fault that I ended up in this strange place?' I managed to gasp.

My brain frying!

Who exactly is Jakeman?

'Yes, yes. It's high time you knew. *Phew!* Let's stop for a rest and I can explain, as far as I know, exactly what happened and how you got here.'

Brilliant, I thought, taking the water bottle from my rucksack and handing it to the funny little man. At last I'm going to learn the truth. Where I am; why Mum can't hear me when I phone her; why, when I've been away for hundreds of years, I still only look eight years old!

'Well,' said Jakeman, taking a swig of water. 'It was like this . . . Whoa, what's that?' he cried suddenly, dropping the bottle in terror. I looked down at his foot and gasped. A strong, hairy hand had emerged from the desert sands at our feet and had grabbed Jakeman by the ankle.

'Oh Charlie, help!' he cried, as the hand started to pull him down into the sand. He had already sunk up to his waist and I grabbed hold of his arms to try and pull him out. It was no good; whatever was on the other end of him was a lot stronger than me.

'I can't hold you, Mr Jakeman,' I yelled as he disappeared up to his shoulders.

'Charlie,' he cried. 'Remember this . . .' but with a final tug, the thing beneath the sands pulled Jakeman below the surface and he completely disappeared!

'Oh no! Come back, Mr Jakeman. Come back!' I yelled. I couldn't believe it; I was alone in the middle of a desert and the only man who could tell me how to get home, had just been swallowed up by the sands. I had to find him; I just HAD to find Jakeman!

I fell to my knees and dug my arms into the sand where he had been, then pushed aside with a swimming motion. There was nothing there. I dug deeper. Still there was nothing, so I took the crocodile's tooth from my rucksack and, using it as a trowel, dug deeper and deeper and deeper into the sand. Finally, I heard a clang as the tooth struck something hard.

Hurriedly, I brushed away the remaining sand, revealing a domed metal lid with a handle on one side, like this:

A domed metal lid

I crouched down and pulled with both hands. The lid opened easily, revealing the mouth of a tube that led straight down into the ground.

Down The Tubes

I lowered myself feet-first into the tube, hoping that I might feel a foothold, but the inside of the tube was completely smooth. So I placed one foot either side of the pipe and then eased my arms over the rim. Immediately, I started to drop, but the braking effect of my rubber-soled trainers slowed my descent just enough. Soon though, my legs started to ache like billy-o as I continued to keep them pressed against the inside of the tube.

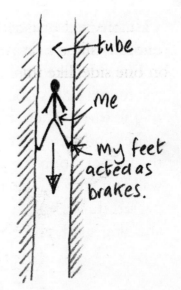

Down I dropped; down, down, down through the dark until I lost all track of time. Then bright flares of light started to pierce the darkness. They flashed and changed colour, from white to red, then blue, green and yellow. Faster and faster they flickered until it felt as if I was falling through the middle of a crazy rainbow. Then everything went black again, and on a sudden updraft of air, I started to slow down. By the time I reached the bottom I was almost floating, and landed on hard ground, amazingly without a bump.

I was in a dark tunnel, carved from solid bedrock. It was almost pitch black, and I strained my ears to try and hear anything, but it was completely silent. All I could hear was the blood rushing in my ears.

Finding the torch in my rucksack, I followed the tunnel as it sloped deeper into the bowels of the earth. Then, in the distance, I could hear noises and I crept even more carefully along the tunnel. Soon I came to a crack in the tunnel wall and with my heart beating fast with fear, I peered through the gap and saw the most amazing sight.

Oh my goodness!

Subterranean Denizens

By the light of a thousand oil lamps I could see a horde of creatures moving about, digging into the rock and carrying away piles of rubble in hand carts.

The creatures looked half-human and half-ape, with wide powerful shoulders and thick muscular arms matted with coarse hair. Their faces were fierce and heavy-browed and when they snarled in their efforts to smash the rocks with their crude instruments, they exposed a row of large and pointed teeth. I scanned the thronging mass, but couldn't see any sign of Jakeman.

It was incredible; these creatures looked almost like Neanderthal men. Perhaps I had discovered a lost stone-age tribe that everyone thought had been extinct for thousands of years. Big deal! I thought, for I hadn't discovered any sign of Jakeman. Oh, blooming heck, this was terrible! What was I going to do next?

I started to panic but knew I must calm down and get my thoughts in some sort of order. Looking around to make sure I was quite safe, I squatted at the back of a deep alcove and fished out my journal. Perhaps writing up my latest adventures would help me think more clearly.

Now that I'm finished, I feel a lot calmer, and I must continue to look for Jakeman. I've got to find him if I'm ever to discover my way home, and as long as I keep away from those scary-looking creatures I should be safe. Then, as I crawled out of the alcove, I felt something under my foot. Bending down, I picked up a pair of oily goggles. Jakeman's goggles. So he had been here! Perhaps he was in the next cave after all, and I had overlooked him in the crowd. I crept across the passage and pressed my face against the narrow crack, to check.

'RARRR!' All of a sudden a hideous face popped up on the other side of the crack in the wall. It was one of the Neanderthal ape-like things.

I'VE BEEN SPOTTED!

HELP!

A Desperado Dictionary

Amigo — Friend.

Bangtail — Wild horse.

Bellyache — Complain.

Bushwhack — Ambush.

Chow — Food.

Chuck — Food!

Critter — Creature, or a
no good person.

Dude — A city slicker.

Hooks — Spurs.

Hang fire — Wait.

Lariat - A rope or lasso.

Lily liver — A coward.

Lingo — language.

Outlaw — A bandit.

Pard — Partner.

Ramuda — A herd of horses.

Red-Eye — Whiskey.

Saddle bum — A sort of cowboy tramp or drifter.

Six shooter — A pistol.

Stampede — A runaway herd.

Tack — A cowboy's working gear.

Vamos — 'Let's get out of here!'

Wrangler — A cowboy.

Questions I would like
some answers to:

① Where am I?
② How did I get here?
③ Which way is home?
④ Why is it always the
same time whenever
I ring home?
⑤ Who is Jakeman?
⑥ Why do his inventions
always help me?
⑦ Does he really know ~~how~~
now I can get home?
⑧ Where can I find Jakeman